CW00517047

The
Stealth Inspector

Phil Rossall

1

The Stealth Inspector

All profits from the sale of this book go to the

Motor Neurone Disease Association

Published March 2023

Copyright © Phil Rossall 2023

ISBN: 9798385930852

To my darling wife, Brenda, who made this book possible.

With thanks to Dave Edwards of Northill Video for suggesting I write a novel and for designing the cover

Author's note: It's not Barnstaple.

Foreword

This book is an amazing achievement. Phil wrote it whilst in the advanced stage of Motor Neurone Disease.

He started it in January 2022 when, already bedbound, the only muscles still working were his thumbs and eyelids. Over the course of the year, he gradually lost the use of his thumbs and needed to resort to blinking to finish this book.

But this novel has nothing to do with MND. It is fundamentally a true story. Only the people, the narrative and the places have been changed. There is no resemblance to anyone living or dead now.

Anyone who's ever been a teacher or a pupil in a school should definitely read this!

The Stealth Inspector

Contents

Chapter 1 - Is that even a thing?

Cons are real. Piracy is real. Conspiracy is not. At least, it may exist in practice, but in theory it's as crazy as a smashed patio. If the all-pervasive propaganda machines of Russia and China can't mount a decent conspiracy, how can the bungling British establishment hope to succeed in pulling the wool over our eyes while convincing us we're not wearing a balaclava? Within a week, our media would be quoting whistle blowers and sources close to government spilling the beans on Woolgate. After that, none but the most dyed-in-the-wool conspiracy theorists would be left desperately clinging on to the raft, and it would only be a matter of time before the lizard people of Buckingham Palace made an appearance.

But the conspiracy that Danny Duckworth suspected was going on, was a fish of a very different colour. Not that its colour was the thing that haunted his working life and stalked his dreams at night. It was the faint but unmistakable odour of oily mackerel which was driving him to distraction. Why the hell could no one else pick it up? The scent that was slowly sending Danny into the welcoming arms of madness was not coming from some cabal perched on top of society, but from a hidden shoal of marine creatures swimming just below the sonar.

The job had not always been this frustrating. For an idealist like Danny, it had started with a burst of unalloyed joy. Even after twenty years, he had not lost any of his enthusiasm or belief in the cause. He was proud that he had been there for that inaugural meeting, proud of being one of the founding fathers present at the birth of Ofsted.

The Office for Standards in Education was conceived in hope and born out of political paranoia. Academics like Professor Duckworth - that is, educational theorists well to the right of sensible - believed that teachers and schools should be held accountable for their performance, in as transparent a manner as possible.

Danny had risen without trace through the ranks of secondary education, from lowly French teacher through Headteacher and Local Authority Adviser to Professor of Education and Transformational Didactics at the University of East Anglia. Along the way, he had amassed a double helping of chips on each shoulder.

To be fair, Danny Duckworth also had visiting professorships. One in Shrewsbury, which seemed to consist of attending two banquets a year and giving a short address before the annual firework display, where the great and not so good in Shropshire society could watch a healthy chunk of their government grant go up in smoke. He had a similar title at Loughborough University, where he contributed to the training of PE teachers at the

National Sports Education Institute, better known as Neanderthal High.

If Danny had his fingers in lots of pies, he was not the only one. Sitting round the table in one of the Cabinet Office briefing rooms were several academics like himself. There was the galloping major, Professor Tim Badloss, a man of no discernible talent except the ability to sniff out a free dinner at three hundred yards. Next to him sat Professor Hans Fuchs, minor TV celebrity and polymath, majoring in self-promotion. It's probably best not to mention his nickname, although people who have had the misfortune to encounter Hans and his unique brand of leaden repartee say it is rather appropriate.

Danny didn't recognise most of the others, but he spotted Sir Zahir "Tickbox" Khan, a local politician who was often seen promoting government initiatives. "And there's that mercenary bastard Hughes from Birmingham" Danny thought, "the government's tame Headteacher, the greatest Tory ever sold."

A quick round-the-table introduction yielded five civil servants, including the head of the Civil Service Sir Gus O'Driscoll, known to everyone in Whitehall as GOD or Lord of the Files. There were a few lobby-fodder MPs and two junior ministers from the Department of Health, one revelling in the title of Minister for Youth Deprivation and Obesogenic Environments. Apparently the latter really is a thing, so it is probably wise to avoid certain housing estates if you don't want to catch fat.

There were several names Danny didn't pick up, but it was too late now. In swept the rather grand figure of the Cabinet Secretary, followed by two children. The great man gave an almost insultingly short dis-pep talk, in which he put this "committee" into the context of the government's plan, giving it the role of providing the "intellectual evidence to underpin the whole . . . er . . . thingie". Having ascertained that this event provided no photo opportunities, he quickly left the group in the hands of GOD.

You could just about tell that Sir Gus felt he was slumming it here, but that didn't stop him applying his ferocious intellect to the matter in hand. In line with Cabinet Office tradition, the meeting was to start with an impartial research analysis. As head of the Civil Service, Sir Gus made it clear that he did not approve of giving this task to people specifically chosen because they knew nothing about the subject. Civil servants would have done a much better job, he implied, as he politely introduced the Cabinet Office's latest BYTs (Bright Young Things).

Today's presenters were not children, although they had been until recently. Stu and Zara were students. One from Oxford and one from Cambridge, strictly in the interests of balance. Zara came across as a confident young woman, not at all fazed by being the only female in the room. She said she was taking History at Cambridge, as if it was some sort of prize. Stu was an altogether different can of worms. In a whiny voice several octaves higher than Zara's, he proclaimed that he too was "taking", in his case PPE at Jesus. He made it sound like some sort of sordid drug which, in a way, it probably was. Danny thought Stu had an eminently slappable face. Both students were clearly high flyers and had the added advantage of having been to public schools, which sounded something like St Vitus's Academy and Nepotism Hall. This had given them extra brownie points on their Cabinet Office's neutrality checklist, as any new inspection regime specifically excluded private education. It was, in the words of one Education Minister "all about schools for oiks".

Danny had to admit, these whizz-kids certainly knew how to put together a decent presentation. They seemed to be intimately acquainted with Powerpoint and all its little widgets.

As an educator, the good professor had to admire the way they interwove visuals and scripted speech. The commentary sounded convincing enough, at least to start with. Stu put his thumbs into the pockets of his waistcoat, which was part of his ensemble. Unfortunately, the three-piece suit looked more like a three-piece suite. Together with the antique pocket watch and the distressed brogues, he resembled a Dickensian slum landlord, probably not the look he was going for. His summary of the history of school inspection and the "legislative landscape" was succinct, as was Zara's piece on the PISA Study and this country's standing in the international rankings of educational achievement, which could be summed up as nowhere near the Singaporeans but comfortably ahead of the Yanks.

All of this served to confirm Danny's own Narrow Boat theory of educational reform. He argued that the countries where children's attainment was highest were the ones where the system had changed the least. For instance, Germany had a method for evaluating pupil attainment which was frankly laughable, but the fact that it was still unchanged after eons of use meant that parents and relatives were on board, because they too were subjected to the same system when they were at school. In Professor Danny's analogy, they were the barges ploughing their painfully slow way down the middle of the canal. Our own education system was more adaptive to modern trends and to the latest political dogma. In contrast to the serene progress of the lumbering barges, Danny was uncomfortably reminded of his one and only attempt at steering a narrowboat on the Grand Union Canal. It had taken a good deal of courage for Danny to ask to take the tiller, and all went well to start with. He made a slight correction to the right and for a while nothing happened. Eventually, the front of the boat, which seemed so ridiculously far away, started to veer to the right like a demented Thatcherite. He thought he had been careful to move the tiller as little as possible, but he was now heading straight for the right bank. A few minuscule corrections later, the boat was slaloming wildly from one towpath to the other before drifting sideways across the canal and coming to an ignominious stop in some overhanging trees. Even now, the memory brought him out in a cold sweat, but he believed that the experience of wild swings and uncontrollable panic had given him the perfect analogy for our record of educational reform.

Danny's musings had rekindled his hopes for today's meeting and he smiled at the mental image of himself standing confidently at the helm of HMS Pedagogia. Unfortunately, he had missed the big reveal of the Scoping Spreadsheet. It did not take him long to catch up, though. The Wunderkinder had summarised the "scale of the problem" by creating an "interactive database of all the education providers under the aegis of the Schools Division of the Department for Education". This created quite a stir in the room, and someone piped up "Do you mean all the schools in England?". After a quick glance at Zara, Stu nodded. He looked happy to move on to demonstrating how the information could be analysed by "interrogating the data and generating powerful graphs and heat maps ". This was greeted by stunned silence, which Danny presumed was in admiration of Stu's ability to fit so many random words into one sentence.

But Mr Piper-Up was not finished with the previous question yet. "I see that you have colour coded the Primary and Secondary schools. Have you done the same with Middle schools?" Stu flashed Zara a look which clearly meant "What the hell are Middle schools?" and she in turn looked imploringly at the chairman, but Sir Gus made a show of ignoring her worthy of any French waiter.

"Can I get back to you on that one?" she asked, making a note on her note pad. "Rookie mistake" thought Danny "I hope you've got plenty of paper".

"Does this cover army schools?" demanded the Galloping Major.

"And faith schools?" someone added unhelpfully.

The BYT-baiting continued for some time, until one participant went too far. A Geordie voice came from the back of the room.

"Where's Berwick? What have you done with Berwick?"

"I thought that was in Scotland" Stu mumbled miserably.

Danny started to feel genuinely sorry for the two students. It was not their fault they were pitched into this bear pit so woefully underprepared. They had just discovered the fatal flaw in the Cabinet Office's thinking. Danny was genuinely impressed at the knowledge the two of them had amassed on their near-vertical learning curves. They had applied innovative techniques to the analysis and presentation of some rather dry data. On the downside, their obvious lack of experience was always going to be a weakness. Even this difficult audience was willing to cut them some slack. But the whole enterprise was doomed to failure by one simple thing: they didn't know what they didn't know.

The Lord of the Files was quick to restore order and the debate on the key issues ensued, with everything "going through the chair". Danny was delighted with the way the discussion went. There was a consensus in the room that English schools needed a national inspection regime and that they were the very people to design it. Danny was making copious notes in his own excitable manner when he heard his name being called out.

The two civil servants from Education were picking their teams, as if this were some sort of Sunday afternoon kick-about. Any annoyance about being taken for granted disappeared as soon as Danny realised he now had everything he wanted. There were to be two "expert working parties" coming from today's meeting and they would "advise ministers and officials on key aspects of the overall plan", which sounded to Danny's fevered brain as if they were trying to keep their clothes clean.

One of the two key aspects was called Standards and Parameters for Yearly Inspections, which was immediately, if somewhat inaccurately, shortened to

SPY. A panel of six expert advisers would be chaired by one of the civil servants.

The other work stream revelled in the name School And Teacher Assessment Norms, but no one could suggest a suitable acronym for it. This was the team Danny had been assigned to. He was itching to get started by telling his five new team mates and their Education Department referee that the idea of annual inspections was a non-starter. He felt slightly disappointed when they all agreed with him, but nothing could touch his state of euphoria. He was now officially an expert adviser to HM Government. His role seemed perfectly positioned at the interface of schools and what he liked to think of as the real world. Then their working party chairman Alec Pryke pointed out the section of their starter pack labelled "Reimbursement of minor expenses and secretarial/research support costs". Danny saw the "minor" figure and had to suppress a low whistle.

It was not a wife-changing sum of money, but it was plenty for what Danny Duckworth had in mind. As soon as their meeting had broken up, he made a bee-line for Stu and Zara, who had been too glum to move.

Professor Duckworth beamed his best toothpaste smile and said "Fancy a coffee?".

Chapter 2 – Off the bridle

"What us'm doing 'day 'n, Miss?".

After less than a week in his new school, Phil Rossall had seen through their little game. Not that he could claim any credit for his perspicacity. Lauren made it all too easy for him. It was clearly her turn to act the yokel today, and she wasn't very good at it. The fledgling German teacher wondered if she was very good at anything. He fervently believed that everybody could excel at something, but even a card-carrying optimist like Phil suspected that, in her case, it was unlikely to manifest itself in school.

"It's Sir, not Miss, Lauren. Miss Reeves was last lesson." Virginia Reeves was another newbie, an English teacher with stars in her eyes. "Anyway, what's the 'n near the end for? Is it supposed to be a short form of the word then?"

The Underachiever Brothers guffawed. It was their game in the first place, but if the teacher didn't fall for it, they were quite prepared to laugh at Lauren instead. Phil noticed that the Swots looked relieved but the Dumplings remained stubbornly unresponsive.

After this opening exchange, the lesson had meandered its way through the September heatwave and drifted away to the high noon of lunch. The weather was not supposed to be hot and dry in this part of the world, where houses were just as damp and green on the inside as they were on the outside. Until now, some of the younger children had assumed that people always smoked when they talked, and that the main difference

11

between cars and cows was that the latter had exhausts at both ends.

But it was not the climate or the teaching that was troubling Phil as he delved into his Boiled to Submission Beef and All-You-Can-Cook Mash. His problem was with geography, and had nothing to do with teaching. In fact, only a few years ago, teenage Phil been so keen on geography that he had not taken it at A-level. He may not have been an expert, but if he had a map in his hand, he could always tell you exactly where he was and where he was going. He had now been living here for three weeks and he had eight maps. If anything, he was less sure about his whereabouts than he was before. If you lived in a county and you were employed by a County Council, it would be nice to know which county that was. So far, the answer had been as clear as the muddy river Yeorn.

The ex-market town of Oxbridlesturridge was indeed on the maps, but it might as well not have been. For a start, its spelling was modal. Over the years, the names of its two constituent hamlets Oxbridle and Sturridge Episcopi had coalesced into one. Some older maps still had it as two places. Some referred to them as Oxgirdle or Slurridge, or both.

However, on three things there was a bit more clarity. Firstly, the word Episcopi should no longer be used, as it referred to a monastery founded in the twelfth century by the French bishop of Conques, who was known locally as Bishop Bignose. The monastery was in truth only a large house, which mysteriously morphed four hundred years later into the "ancestral" home of the Sincorazon family, whose coat of arms depicted a chain mail clad knight with his feet on his mangled foe. The

12

victor held a bloody sword in one hand and a dripping heart in the other. Their motto was the Spanish phrase "Su Casa Mi Casa", your house is my house. They claimed to have been here generations before the Armada, when they changed their name to Hartles. The Guildhall still displayed the meticulously forged documents.

Most people also agreed that the town was in Devon, but that it was surrounded by Somerset, which led Oxbridlesturridgeans to describe it as an island. Strictly speaking, it was a Devonian enclave, or exclave, depending on your point of view. Either way, this isolation had bred a siege mentality among the "Townies". After centuries of French and Spanish rule, the town was fervently Catholic, in contrast to the surrounding villages, which tended towards the Nonconformist. Fortunately, the Church of England had all of that covered. History also had an effect on the local dialect, which could best be described as El Rey's English. This had a considerable impact on the only secondary school in the area, which also had to cater for the children from the neighbouring farms and villages, who spoke a sort of sawn-off Mummerset. An interesting place for a linguist to live, one might think. But in stark contrast to his current and future colleagues, Phil was no linguist. He was a language teacher.

However, on one thing everybody could agree: the town's name was pronounced Oxbridge.

That had not stopped one mis-lexic wit scrawling on the extra-large roadsigns "Wellcome to Sandwitch City, home of the Inbred". Phil thought it was probably the work of one of the sixth formers that Hartles School and

Community College was not supposed to have, but it could just as easily have been the mayor.

Phil had fallen in love with the place the first time he had laid eyes on it, which was barely two weeks after he received the job offer. At the time, Phil had no experience of interviews, but even he thought it was odd to be given a job sight unseen, particularly a Scale 2 junior management role commonly known as a Tuppence On Top. His PGCE supervisor at Durham University called it "irregular" which, for her, was pretty strong language. It was particularly awkward, because she had been the one who had recommended the weekend course at Dartington Hall in the south of Devon, where the unorthodox approach had been made.

"It's a mini-course for high flyers, but they haven't been able to fill it. So, you could go instead" she had told him encouragingly. "All expenses are covered by the government's Hothousing scheme. It's an amazing place, so it won't be a completely wasted weekend."

She hadn't had to write any references for him, so she knew he was at a loose end. He preferred to think of what he was doing as a gap year, an opportunity to travel and work his way around the world for a year, although he wasn't so sure about the working bit. When his studies in Durham had finished, he did not hoist his backpack and disappear into the blue yonder. So far, he hadn't even done the planned day trip to Barnard Castle, which was apparently a must-see. In his final teaching practice, he had done more than enough coach travel to last a lifetime, commuting between Stockton-on-Tees and civilisation.

The Stealth Inspector

The more Phil found out about Dartington Hall, the more he wanted to go there. Medieval half-timbered buildings, comfortable bedrooms, great food and its own pub. It all sounded pretty good to a student whose bones needed thawing out after months of living in a glacial Durham bedsit. His walk to the University led him through a slice of the Wear valley and past the cathedral. It may have been the closest you could get to heaven on earth, but it made him wonder whether a centrally heated hell would be such a bad idea. The prospect of riverside walks through the balmy meadows of south west England was rather appealing.

The train journeys had been fun, as had the ridiculously sun-drenched stroll across London to Paddington station. On the train, Phil tried to spot any budding teaching geniuses, but the hothouse flowers did not show themselves. He might as well not have bothered. As soon as he got off, he saw the Dartington bus. This was no public transport vehicle, and it hadn't been for a good fifty years. It was hard to miss, as were the six young people strolling nonchalantly towards it. Phil wondered which one of the seven dwarves he was going to be. Dopey, presumably. Then he recognised Archie Spargel. "Quite an oversight, Mr Disney" thought Phil "not having a dwarf called Loathsome".

Despite the presence of Spargel, the hothouse atmosphere seemed to suit Phil. It was so far removed from the everyday realities of school teaching as to allow his chaotic imagination to go wherever it wanted. He really enjoyed all the lectures and roleplaying tasks devised by the Education Department in London and delivered by Devon County Council. Even better,

15

The Stealth Inspector

Smarmy Archie kept a low profile which, in Phil's view, was still about ten feet too high.

The keynote speech sounded intriguing. Phil didn't know what to make of the title. What was "The transparent school. Re-envisioning parents in the light of the consumer revolution" when it was at home? Other questions occurred to Phil. What could the lecture possibly have to do with seven high flying modern languages teachers (or rather six high flyers plus Phil)? Were "transparent" schools meant to be see-through, or did it refer to the parents' self-identified gender? And who the hell was Professor Danny Duckworth?

At the end of the presentation, "Call me Danny" asked for questions. Phil could not very well pose any that had occurred to him beforehand, even though only one issue had been resolved: transparent really did mean see-through.

During the lecture and the drinks that followed, Phil could not shake off the feeling that the professor only had eyes for him. Phil had never experienced anything similar before, and he didn't like it one bit. He was not surprised when Danny sat down next to him at dinner. Phil braced himself for another spate of Jargonese. But what he got was a smile which could curdle cream and the words "Have you heard of Oxbridlesturridge?"

He hadn't seen *that* coming.

Chapter 3 - The plan comes together

"You can lead a horse to water, but you can't shove 'n in". Even inside his head, Danny couldn't get his mother-in-law's Cornish accent right. She had a point, though. Was Phil Rossall being deliberately obtuse or was he really that thick? Danny liked to think of himself as a leading academic in the world of education, which made him all the more furious with himself for using the T-word, even in his thoughts. But this was not the time to lose patience. Not after all the good work of Team Danny.

The School Inspection Research Group, to give his team its proper name, was not a recognised entity, but in the halls of academia, it had something much better: funding. To an outsider, 0.5 of a full-time post may not have sounded like a big deal, but it most certainly was. If there was one thing that united Danny's profession, it was frustration at constantly having to take precious time off research in order to apply for funds. If someone offered them an extra fifty percent of their salary for an unspecified time period, Danny thought, they would have bitten their hand off, rings and all.

Professor Duckworth was not a mercenary man. With the approval of the workstream chair Alec Pryke, he had split his allowance into three unequal chunks. Now he could negotiate time out with his employers at the University of East Anglia. He could also pay Stuart and Zara a wage which was the envy of their "uni-mates".

The Stealth Inspector

Zara couldn't believe her luck. She was working fewer hours per week than she previously spent waitressing at the Flirty Pig. This way, she had more time for her own studies, an interesting sideline and a great addition to her CV. Her Machu Pichu fund was flourishing too. She would soon have enough money to do the trip in style, experiencing the wonders of the Andes without the dysentery and the pulmonary embolism.

However, the feeling of liberation was strongest in Stuart. When he realised that he had finished his last essay for the Old Etonians and the Illiterate Eight - the university's elite rowing team - he had "gone a bit mad". He had changed his name and his look. Unfortunately, he had also told his former clients exactly what he thought of them. In fairness, the Old Etonians didn't mind being described as entitled morons. They knew their future was secured, and that when it came to ability, the British establishment was an equal opportunity employer. The rowers were not so keen on being called the Sit Backwards And Pull brigade. No harm done, though. At least, nothing that antibiotics and a stomach pump couldn't sort out.

Danny was very pleased with the progress his team was making. With the benefit of the professor's experience, his minions had corrected their original presentation. The newly re-christened Stuart had recovered from his river baptism, and had started to show Danny exactly what he meant by a powerful interactive tool. Zara was now using it to look for the anomalies in the English school system, which Danny had long suspected were out there. Zara had a rat-trap brain and laser-like focus. He only hoped she would eventually use it in the service of humanity. Failing that, he thought, she'd make a terrific lawyer. It was only a matter of time before she found something big. For now, the one anomaly she had found would do just fine.

The working group set up by the government to oversee the school and teacher assessment norms had its first business meeting in a broom cupboard somewhere in the bowels of Whitehall. For no apparent reason, it was known as the Churchill Tea Room. Danny speculated that it had previously been a storage space for whisky. The same could be said about Sir Winston himself. Danny doubted much tea had been consumed.

Despite its unwieldy name, the working group's task sounded simple: to make sure testing worked. Danny knew that it would be far from simple, which is why he was happy to use its unfortunate acronym SATAN. The devil really was in the detail. Of course, Danny would never say anything like that in public. Neither did it imply anything derogatory. Danny was a true believer, a zealot with a clipboard. But he grew up in Liverpool, so he stuck to the strict code: you never pass up the chance to make a quick joke, or to kick it while it's down.

Stuart and Zara were extremely reluctant to be in the meeting. They were not at all keen on returning so close to the scene of the crime. Stuart tried to argue that the group was meant to have only six experts and a chairman, but he dropped his objection before anyone had the chance to say he wasn't an expert. Danny was insistent, and chairman Alec was delighted to work with his Zara. It turned out that he was her maternal uncle. "Besides" he added cheerfully "old Ironsides Johnstone will not be joining us. He upped and died over the weekend, so there's plenty of room."

"Plenty of room" was not the description Danny would have used. The Tea Room was rammed full of big bodies and even bigger egos. Danny did not include his team in this unflattering picture, and uncle Alec seemed to be chiselled out of sterner stuff. He was so obviously a spy that Danny felt slightly insulted by his brazenness. The way he introduced himself as Pryke, Alec Pryke was a challenge. "Go on, I dare you" he seemed to be saying. He may have been on the verge of retirement, but you wouldn't want to get into a fight with him.

They started the meeting with a round of introductions. This was necessary because only half of the original group was there. Not only had the disability campaigner Sir Frank Johnstone, in Alec's words, "cried off", but two others had graced the committee with their absence. Camilla Anstruthers had to tend to her dahlias and, ever mindful of his civic duty, Tickbox Khan was helping police with their enquiries.

Sitting cramped around the table with Alec and Team Danny were two Headteachers, a recently retired Trades Union leader, an empty suit from the Treasury and a professional Northerner. The last of these was George Bratby, a former shadow minister and MP for Bradford and Scarsdale. His catchphrase was "It's grim up north". Danny was sceptical about this, though. He suspected it was grim everywhere George went.

Nevertheless, Danny was impressed by the strength of the substitutes' bench. The two Headteachers were nothing short of inspirational. Melissa Gray had turned round so many failing Primary schools that it was a wonder she still knew which way North was. The representative of the Secondary sector was none other than Nathan Artharathiwardena, known to all as King

Arthur. He was famous for treating teenagers from a troubled Birmingham estate as if they were all members of court at the Round Table. The children and adolescents loved their roles as knights, dames and maidens. They were expected to act in accordance with the ancient code of chivalry. Amazingly, they did. In class you could hear a sword drop, exam results were stellar and the only problem was a chronic shortage of maidens.

Yet again, Danny had got everything he wanted. The short paper he circulated on "maintaining the integrity of inspection results" had gone down a storm. They all agreed that the whole Ofsted programme needed a robust form of quality control. A system of impartial spot checks seemed to be the obvious way to ensure that inspections were carried out to the same high standards in all schools.

"The last thing we want is to have schools complaining about unfairness" said Danny, going in for the kill, "or appealing against decisions."

In the context of this meeting, this seemed more like overkill. Everyone was sold on the idea of what Danny called "light touch checks and balances". When the Treasury suit realised that light touch meant cheap, his eyes lit up.

"Do you mean like a mystery shopper?" he asked.

"More like spying on the bloody spies" boomed Professional Northerner.

In the silence that ensued, Zara could just about be heard muttering "Ooh, mummy *would* be proud."

While the other members of the working party divided up the mundane tasks, Danny was free to design his grand plan. He knew that they had first to test his theory in a real school where the supervision of teachers was patently inadequate. Hence the search for anomalies, schools that simply didn't add up. Sure enough, Stuart and his trusty computer had found a real beauty. There were so many apparent irregularities associated with Hartles School and Community College, Oxbridlesturridge, that Stuart didn't know where to start. Zara did, though. A few hours of intensive training from Danny and generations of Tinker Tailoring had given her the ideal preparation for smelling this kind of rat. It was simple enough, she thought: get the big picture, then ignore it. Find something that doesn't make sense and pursue it like a bloodhound until it drops to the ground in a quivering heap and then grip it with your teeth until it's shaken to molecules.

Other people would have been satisfied with finding out that the official records didn't know what county the school was in. Even Stuart fell into that category. But Zara was looking for something more specific than that. Something you could see all the way around, so it couldn't be explained away, even by a bullshitting Cabinet minister. And here it was: Hartles had eight classes of German and no German teacher.

When Danny "dropped by" the school for a "courtesy visit", his reception seemed friendly but guarded. The Head was agitated as Danny skirted round the obvious question of who the hell had been teaching the kids German. Danny knew who it was, although he still couldn't believe that the school was committed to starting an A level course in September. But instead of delivering the coup de grace, Professor Duckworth made the Head an offer she really couldn't refuse. A shiny new high-flying German teacher and a small amount of extra funding made this a gift horse worthy of no dental inspection. All Danny had to do was to find someone to fit the bill.

Of course, Danny had someone lined up for the job. It would take a particular, not to say unique, skill set. The ability to teach German to A-level standard, that was the easy bit. Someone who was fully qualified, but hadn't fixed up a job yet at this eleventh hour. Someone idealistic enough to want to work in the backside of beyond, but desperate enough to be enticed by a measly Scale 2. Someone naïve. Someone gullible. Someone like Phil Rossall.

Fortunately for society but unluckily for Danny, there wasn't anyone like Phil Rossall. The professor had devoted a lot of time to the hunt. Zara had spent the weekend as Serving Wench number 2 at Dartington Hall. Danny had also plied Phil with beer until he finally agreed to a telephone interview with the Head the next day at 11am British Hangover Time. Even then, he strung it out for so long that Danny seriously wondered whether it was worth all the effort.

Only then did Danny manage a smile. In this tug of war, there were three teams pulling in different directions: Prof Danny and the Ofsteds, an entire school and, last and most definitely least, the slight figure of Phil Rossall. He could quibble as much as he wanted, he had never stood a chance.

Chapter 4 - Faceplanting

Phil had taken to Oxbridge like a duck to orange. He certainly didn't think of it as Oxbridlesturridge anymore. As he breathed in the fresh green air, the redundant syllables just floated away. Phil already felt he was a true townie and, amazingly, the locals seemed to think so too. His lodgings with Señora Prowse were comfortable and embarrassingly cheap. She seemed to have adopted him as one of her many sons. He had thought that people would be a bit stand-offish in this part of the world, but he still wasn't sure exactly what part that was. It seemed that he only needed a cheery smile and a few words of ungrammatical Spanish to fit right in.

'Buenos, Charlie" he said to the owner of the corner shop, "Guardian please". Charlie's wasn't just a fag and paper shop. It had rows of shelves crammed full with a dizzying assortment of goods. At first, Phil couldn't find a unifying theme, and then the penny dropped: it was all stuff that nobody would ever buy.

The same under-preneurial spirit seemed to pervade the town centre. Phil must indeed have gone native if he thought of this tiny jumble of shops and pubs as the centre of anything. There was a covered space known as the Gallon Market. According to his landlady, it was called that because you could still buy a gallon of potatoes there, assuming you had the foresight to take a gallon bucket with you. Every Thursday and Saturday morning, the farmers from "out around" would pile their produce high and add a helpful sign on which was scrawled "Spud's". The Señora looked wistful as she said "Once they had carrots. Under the mud they looked rather tempting. Of course, no one bought any, so I suppose we will never know."

The town was better known for its Butchers Lane. This was a quaint little street lined with shop windows proudly advertising the name of the butcher and a wide variety of meat. A closer inspection of the windows revealed a few lamb chops and some plastic sprigs of parsley. Phil decided, just for the hell of it, to go into one of the emporia. His choice was completely random, as they all appeared to be identical. He did like the sign above the door, though, which read "J Lees. Purveyors of fine meats since 1865". Phil greeted the shopkeeper with an "Alright?", which was answered with a nod and a "Right". He was getting the hang of this now. The butcher was really a farmer. He was therefore also a villager, no matter how isolated his farm was. Any attempt at a pseudo-Iberian greeting would have been met with stony silence. But he was in the game now and the butcher's eyes conveyed the message "Your go now".

Phil played a conventional gambit "Got any sausages?"

The latest Mr Lees smiled. "Pork or beef?"

"What've you got?" Phil countered hopefully.

"I'll just go and see" said the shopkeeper and then he went. Not into some back storage room but straight out of the front door. Phil stepped out into the lane to watch Mr Lees go in and out, bouncing like a pinball between the other butcher's shops. Phil saw him visit two Ridds, one Proudworthy and another Lees.

When they were both back inside, the butcher smiled and said "I could do you some nice hog's pudding. They say it goes great fried up with some laver bread."

Phil felt the game slipping away from him, but he continued to play it straight. "And where do I get laver bread?" he enquired manfully.

"I hear Blackford Rocks is pretty good. No fatalities this year. "

"Is that how you eat your hog's pudding?" Phil asked unwisely.

"Me, sir, good Lord no " the butcher chuckled. "Us Leeses are all vegetarian."

Now Phil definitely felt he had been pinned in a corner. Mr Lees deftly moved to the door and said over his shoulder as he made a break for the lane "I'll just go and get it then."

Phil was chuckling too. Game, set and check mate to the man in the bloody apron.

This was all very well, but he had promised the Señora that he would cook for her tonight. Phil was pretty handy in the kitchen, but he hadn't yet decided what to make. He doubted that one-and-a-half feet of emulsified pig fat would quite fit the bill. A quick perusal of the other shops yielded little. Casa Julia sold "ladies' couture" that had gone out of fashion with Queen Mary. Its stock also formed the basis for the charity shop next door, where even the knockdown prices failed to attract many buyers of pre-loathed knitwear. Neither Julie nor the Psittacosis Society seemed to be profiting from the situation.

The Stealth Inspector

So Phil did what all the locals did, and with equal reluctance. He went down to the Yorne Quay Industrial Estate to Tommy Lord's supermarket. This was located in a former fertiliser warehouse which had been downcycled for its current use. Fortunately, Tommy was not there today, so there would be none of his traditional service with a snarl. Having created a monopoly by buying up and shutting down the only two groceries in Oxbridge, Tommy Lord embarked on a totally gratuitous advertising campaign. Billboards sprung up overnight sporting Tommy's ravaged mug and the slogan "Lord knows, where else are you going to go?". The townies and the villagers were united in their reaction: he was obnoxious, he was a blasphemer and, most unforgivably, he was from Bristol. The farmers were up in arms. The bloody grockle was selling camembert, bold as brass. But they swallowed their pride, squared their shoulders and entered the devil's pantry. As did Phil. After all, where else was there to go?

His duty done, Phil felt that he had earned a pint. He decided to continue his slow-motion alphabetical pub crawl with a Saturday pint at the Nag's Head. Phil had been intrigued by the pub's swinging sign, which featured a disturbingly naturalistic portrait of a woman.

"Third wife" the landlord explained, before Phil had a chance to ask. "What'll you have? We got 4X and we got Dead Dog. The Dead Dog's off, but that's the way they seem to like it."

Phil had already heard enough stories about the legendary local cider to send him scurrying for the 4X. Glazed-eyed zombies and pickled canines did not feature on his wish list of weekend entertainment. He supped his beer and surveyed the wreck of a carpet. It

27

had seen better decades, but not recently. It was less in
need of a little TLC than a lot of TNT. At least
somebody had kept a sense of humour about it. A sign
by the door said "Please wipe your feet on the way out".

But Sunday had quickly become the highlight of the
week, because it was Yomping Day. Phil had only been
on a couple of yomps so far, and they had been great
fun. He had already learned about tussocking and
bogsnorting. Basically, striding purposefully from one
grassy tussock to another was supposed to be the
quickest way to get across moorland, especially when it
was wet, which was always. If your boot slipped off the
chosen hump of vegetation, the traditional response was
to land face first in the muddiest patch of foul-smelling
bog available. Although still a newcomer, Phil was fast
becoming an expert in this technique.

The origins of the game were lost in the mists of time,
but its current guardian was a young biology teacher
called Steve Jones. Everyone agreed he was a great guy.
His fascination with beetles was curiously infectious and
he was the undisputed king of yomping. He would set
the rendezvous at one of the car parks up in the wilds of
Exmoor and take his little group for a leisurely stroll to a
seemingly random spot in the arse-end of nowhere.
Today, he had enlisted the help of Bobby Chudleigh to
dig a hole three metres square and half a metre deep.
Then everyone scrabbled through the disturbed earth
looking for bugs, which were collected in a large glass jar.
Steve then lovingly called out their Latin names and
counted out how many of each were present in the
sample.

"That's a lot of bugs" said Mop Bucket. In those non-PC
days, he was known as the remedial teacher, although it

would have been hard to think of much he could possibly have remedied. Fortunately, Huw Davies was on hand to play his part as the resident maths genius and tell them roughly how many that would be for the whole of Exmoor.

"That's a lot of bugs" said Phil before he could stop himself.

They carefully replaced the soil, critters and vegetation and sat down squelchily for another rest. Steve showed them his compass and pointed in the direction of today's yomp. He sat down again and they chatted quietly. Then he said "Bullmore Arms" and all hell broke loose.

The rout was led by Bobby C., whose straight-legged wellington lollop reminded Phil of a herd of friesians stampeding towards the feeding trough. But soon the natural order asserted itself, with the alpha yompers deftly tussocking their way over the hill and out of sight. Huw was locked in a lung-busting stride for stride battle with Chalky Dave, the school technician and unhandy-man. Steve was already out of sight in one direction and Phil in the other. The latter was pleased with his progress this week, although he still had an alarming tendency towards the horizontal. By the time he had ploughed his way to the Bullmore Arms, the others were lying on the grassy bank opposite the pub, waiting for him to arrive. He was still unable to speak, but Phil felt a surge of pride: they could not enter the pub without him. The last to arrive bought the beer. He was happy with his role, but still unable to speak.

"Don't worry" said Steve kindly "I'll order and you can pay."

The Stealth Inspector

The Bullimore was an unusual pub, but the home brewed bitter and Sunday roasts were excellent. The food passed the Bobby C test. The plates were hidden under a mound of food.

"And they're proper twelve-inchers too" he proclaimed.

"But it's not size that matters" Chalky teased "it's what you do with it."

"What else can you do with a plate?" Bobby enquired, puzzled.

The Bullmore was off the grid long before it was fashionable. No mains gas, water or electricity, not even a generator. Bottled gas and wood were the only energy sources and there was a well in the middle of the lounge.

"Full of history, this place" said Bobby C, a propos of nothing. "In the seventeenth century, it was the assize of Black Jack Beadle, the Hanging Judge of Exmoor."

"I suppose it was the only place around that wasn't made of sticks and cowshit" mused Huw.

"Only place" whispered Bobby darkly "with a wooden staircase."

They assembled on the other side of the lane and chatted amiably for a while. Steve pointed out the exact direction from which they had come. Thoughts turned to school tomorrow, but without the sense of dread Phil had observed in Stockton-on-Styx.

"I must do some more ticks tonight" said Huw. "I'm already 350 behind target. It's alright for you, Phil. Some parent's bound to spot if I start ticking wrong answers."

The Stealth Inspector

Life was pondered and food digested. Then Steve
shouted "Car park" and dived through the hedge.

Chapter 5 – Pushing up the laver bread

The first assembly of the new school year had put the mog well and truly amongst the doves. It was all new to Phil and Ginny, but there was a palpable sense of puzzlement amongst the rest of the staff. This was not because the headmistress Señora Hartles was taking assembly. It had become a tradition that the Jefe would address the whole school at the start of the year, and not be seen again by most of the children before Christmas. The head cut an unimposing figure, painfully thin and shy, as she mumbled her script into the lectern. She had never really got the hang of the job since she had inherited the head-dom from her uncle Caney Jim Hartles twelve years before. All eyes turned to the deputy head and town mayor Peter Smythe, who reassured them with a smile and a pacifying hand gesture which clearly meant "Don't worry, I'll explain it all later." Peter needed all his amateur dramatic skills, which ran the whole gamut from Gilbert to Sullivan, to maintain a calm façade. What the hell was the Jefe on about?

The head's address had started traditionally enough with the school's annual score card. "Oxford and Cambridge 5 Dartmoor 4" she mumbled. That was pretty much the epitome of a successful year for the school. But then the speech had started to go off the rails in a most un-Hartles manner. Alien words cropped up, like attainment, performance and targets. Who had written this tosh for her? Then some idiot passed her a microphone which, in another breach of Hartles tradition, was actually working. A collective "d'uh" rose up, briefly accompanied by rolling of the eyes and gnashing of the teeth. How the hell was that going to speed the daft bat up? The senior students were looking particularly uncomfortable sitting on the gritty parquet, as Uncle Peter Smythe had requested, "legs akimbo". He had told the Year 5 Vasquez girls on the front row to spread themselves. In private, they could titter all they liked about Uncle Pete's unintentional double entendres, but there was never so much as a stifled snort in his presence.

There were many reasons why Uncle was revered and adored by everyone in this tiny town but, as he freely conceded, "being the eldest of thirteen smythlings doesn't do any harm." If one of the kids had seriously transgressed, there came a knock at the door that evening and there stood Uncle Pete, saying that he had popped round for a quick chat. With the family sitting round the front room over a cup of tea, Tio Pepe, as he was affectionately known, would talk about the weather and the latest bit of Town gossip. At some point in the brief visit, Mayor Smythe would fix the culprit with a steely stare which clearly conveyed the message "shall I tell your parents or will you?" Generally, that was enough. Many of the parents had themselves been the victims of a quick chat, and the others knew the score as well. After a cordial farewell, Pete would say in a stage whisper "I'll see myself out". A few steps from the front door, he would stop and listen to the sound of screaming voices and thrown furniture.

The day before the Weird Assembly had been an equally odd in-service training day. With the benefit of hindsight, some of the old lags could see a connection

between the INSET day and what they had just
experienced in school, which was another first for
Hartles. To be accurate, it was only a Half Baker Day, a
name which appealed to Phil's sense of poetic irony. But
there were gasps of disbelief when they found out that
the second half day would take place this Saturday on
the isle of Lundy. The initial outrage at having to give up
weekend time for a school do was tempered with excited
curiosity. Gerry Mee - known to everyone in the school
as the other deputy - had just dropped this bombshell
when the questions started to rain down. He glanced
across at the Señora for help, but who was he kidding?

"Will there be leisure time on the island?"

"Enough time for the round island yomp?" asked Steve
excitedly.

"Will the pub be open?" 'added one wit, to raucous
laughter. Who was going to close it?

"Who's paying for all of this?"

"It's a gift from Don Ron" Gerry said reverently.

"So he does exist" quipped Crispy Dave.

Sir Ronald Hartles did indeed exist, but he only
ventured out of Hartles Hall to go to the local airstrip. In
the absence of any evidence to the contrary, he was
known as the only agoraphobic skydiver in the West.

The rest of the meeting was taken up with admin and
handover chats. These gave the people taking over
classes a chance to find out about them from their
previous teachers. This was particularly valuable for new
staff if, in Phil's case, a little surreal. For most, the
conversation went something like:

The Stealth Inspector

"Page 93, watch Boucher and Ridd"

"Which Ridd?"

"2 and 5"

Hartles had very few behavioural problems, and the small number of troubled families they did have to deal with were from remote farms and villages out and around, where mercifully the default child type was dumpling. Many of these were called Ridd, but it was only the offspring of Jan Ridd who could be bothered to export their troubles to others. The problem was that there were so many of them. Jan still housed grown-up children from his first two marriages and Mother Earth had brought her unruly brood with her to Ridd Mires. And then they had sextuplets. By this time, they had run out of names, so the children were known as One to Six. Mother Earth had recently become a grandmother at the age of 34. No one knew how many children Jan had sired outside of wedlock, but his neighbours' verdict was unanimous: "Jan Ridd. Not much of a farmer but one hell of a fertiliser."

But Jan was as wily as a fox and he had the morals of an MP. He soon grasped that there would never be a profit from farming. What he had was a remote and beautiful location between Exmoor and the sea. He also had a silver mine and a seemingly bottomless supply of hangers-on aged from four to forty-four. So, he sold all his livestock and specialised in three things: benefit claiming, adventure tourism and pornography.

Jan had so many kids knocking about the place that application-writing for state benefits was a time-consuming but lucrative affair. He had discovered early on that every child was a little earner, and that twenty-four could live as cheaply as twelve.

The adventure tourism business was surprisingly successful. The campsite attracted young people with a thirst for adventure. Hiking, sea kayaking and coasteering were all readily available, and the mine was a popular attraction. Silver mining had once been widespread along the Exmoor coast, but it had never really been commercially viable. However, being able to dig for your own silver and keep whatever you found was proving a great draw for the campsite. With the price of the precious metal going through the roof, some happy campers had returned from their holiday with more money than when they started. This was no skin off Jan's nose. For him it was easy money with virtually no overheads.

The search for a winter-time money-spinner took a little longer, but Jan was delighted with his choice. He had always fancied himself as a movie director, and West Country Love Inc. gave him a chance to be a film producer as well. His films combined the usual pornographic clichés with stunning scenery, a sort of Hollywood with hypothermia. So far, the films were selling well, especially The MILFs Of Sexmoor and Debbie Does Dunster.

Was it any wonder, Phil's colleagues asked each other, that the younger Riddlets had grown into such chaotic children? They were careful not to say this in public, though. Jan Ridd was vice-chairman of the school's governors.

Phil's "quick chats" were anything but quick, and he soon found out that they were not going to be chats either.

The Stealth Inspector

Phil had to sit through two hours of theatrical declamations, at the end of which he was about minus ten the wiser. But Phil had inherited all but one of his classes from Doktor Doktor Liesl von Ruebesch-Strelitz. Here at last was the German teacher Hartles never had.

The reason Stuart and Zara couldn't find her on the books as a teacher was that she was down as Secretarial and Support Staff. Her roles included mail sorter, first aid trainer, feminine hygiene counsellor, exam invigilator, cleaner and dinner lady, although Liesl preferred "ladies who lunch".

"Call me Liesl, daahling" she told Phil "but don't call me Doktor. In Vienna, we don't get out of bed for just one Doctor." In return, she called everyone "daahling", including the head and, on one memorable occasion, the Queen. Her Majesty's reaction was to cast her eyes to the ground around their feet and say "Oh, I thought one of the corgis had got out."

However, Liesl's eccentricities were most immediately apparent in her dress sense, if sense was the right word. Human bodies come in a variety of shapes, but cuboid is not normally one of them. Around her battleship frame Liesl had wound a sea of cashmere, topped off with a fur stole and a pound shop tiara. Phil found out later that the diamonds were real but not valuable, and that the stole he thought was roadkill was in fact two minks caught in the act of eating each other's backside. Quite why someone would want this circle of death round their neck was a mystery to Phil.

However, what had gone wrong with the German classes last year was no longer a mystery to him. Two days before the start of the school year, Father Arnold

Steinhauer, the German teacher, took his dog Benbo for a walk along the North Cliffs to clear away the cobwebs. They had just got to the Devil's Cauldron when Benbo disappeared. Father Arnold leaned over the edge and saw a tabby kitten scrabbling across the sheer cliff face, pursued by the Father's Jack Russell. Then a big chunk of rock and soil decided it didn't want to be part of the cliff any more, taking the corpulent priest along for the ride.

As with so many things in life, the Greeks have the right phrase for it. English speakers compare a heavy downpour to raining cats and dogs, but a Greek would think "Lightweights. In proper cloudbursts it rains priests." So much heavier and more satisfying, thought Phil.

Father Arnold's vertical visit to the Devil's Cauldron had left Hartles School with a big problem. Six classes were expecting German lessons to start in three days' time and no teacher could be found for love nor money. Gerry Mee, the other deputy head, was at his wit's end, not that he was ever all that far away from it. He couldn't very well have them all playing croquet for two hours a week. Then he thought of Liesl. "Nah" he said aloud, and he was right. Looking back over the year, maybe croquet hadn't been such a bad idea.

"Oh, I didn't *teach* anyone" Liesl declared in response to Phil's obvious question. "I am not qualified. We learned to kiss hands and sing *Wien, Wien oh du allein*. We did projects on the great psychoanalysts and Sachertorte,"

By the time the "handover" had finished, they had missed Gerry's briefing on tomorrow's Chaos Day, but they did know that the music was the Helston Floral Dance.

Chapter 6 - Bobbing gin palace

The mighty Mississippi river is many things to many people. But one thing that it definitely is not is the Atlantic Ocean. Neither is the river Clyde, where the last of the paddle steamers, the Waverley, was born. Alright, thought Professor Danny Duckworth, I know ships aren't born, but it was hard to think clearly amid all the pitching and yawing, rolling and hurling. Especially the hurling. His fevered mind seemed incapable of ordering his thoughts. Was yawing even a word? What was a scouser like him doing in this Godforsaken corner of the world? And what kind of a lunatic would take a paddle steamer out into the Bristol Channel?

"Nice weather for it" said Uncle Peter Smythe. Danny had been focusing on the horizon and had not seen Peter coming. "Hola Pepe" replied Danny, diving straight into the vernacular. He had been in Oxbridge for the worst part of a week now, and Uncle Pete had been the only chink of light. And a very significant chink as well. He had rescued Danny from his cell at Pawsey's Hotel and Cattery. He had shown him out and around, even taking him to Ridd Mires to meet Mother Earth and sample one of her magic mushroom pies, which gave a whole new meaning to high tea. Mother Earth was Pete's cousin, but then who wasn't?

Mayor Pete also took him to his local pub, the Spit and Sawdust. When Danny enquired about the name, Pete answered wistfully "Those were the days. When they could afford sawdust." He gave him a shot glass of Dead Dog cider and said "You don't want more than that. It

40

tends to make your internal organs try to be external." Danny didn't even want that much, but he realised that he was being tested. This was some sort of initiation ceremony, and failure was not an option. He raised his glass, stopped when he got within a few inches of his nose, tossed his head back and thought of Croxteth. "Is it dead poodle?" he gasped, resting his head on the bar. "French or toy?" quizzed the landlord. "Toy" said Danny, slumping off his stool. "Blimey, he's right" exclaimed the landlord. "He's the first one to get it right since Flambé Jack." "Who's that?" enquired Danny from the floor. Pete replied, helping him up. "That's him in the corner", indicating a deeply ravaged man. "Flambé Jack, the human warning." Danny just had to ask "what warning?" Pete grimaced "Not to drink the stuff close to the fire."

It was a short time, but Danny and Pete had become firm friends. Danny's motivation was clear. Mayor Smythe was a valuable asset, a gift from the gods. He was fast becoming a major cog in the professor's machine. He was also good fun, a source of entertainment and a ray of sunshine in this benighted town.

Pete's thought processes were harder to fathom, and he wasn't a great one for introspection. He belonged to Oxbridge and Oxbridge belonged to him: town, out and around, the whole four yards. He had all the power he had ever wanted, he held the place in the palm of his calloused hand, and he was bored. He was tired of the constant jokes about pigshit and incest, tired of all the self-satisfied mediocrity, tired of her indoors. It felt good to show off his little kingdom to an outsider, someone he was not related to. Danny seemed just the man to shake the place up a bit. Pete told the Prof bluntly that he "didn't give a flying fig about education." Then he quickly added "Don't get me wrong, I love my school. And I firmly believe that every child is a potential human being. You've convinced me that you have kids' interests at heart. So let's not hear another word about edu-bloody-cation".

Danny was just about to ask what they should talk about when Pete stood up and said cheerfully "Let's go bowling". Danny enquired about shoe hire, to which Pete replied "I believe hobnails are the footwear of choice, but you'll be fine. It's not your American ten-pin bowling. It's more like skittles on crack". Uncle Pete took a careful swig of his Dog. "And don't put your fingers in the balls, Mrs Worthington."

Pete carefully covered his glass with a pre-soaked beermat and passed it to the landlord. "Better leave it at that" he said. "I've got to drive next Tuesday". Danny counted fourteen steps to the front door of the Swan and Railway. "Two things this town doesn't have" Pete replied to a question Danny hadn't yet formulated. He wasn't at all surprised when Uncle Pete spurned the pub's front door and turned sharp right into a pitch-black alley. Danny didn't see the low metal gate until he had somersaulted over it. His guide shushed him and whispered "Flood defences". Danny probably looked puzzled, but it was too dark to tell. "But we're on top of a bleeding hill" he objected. "I know" came the proud response "second highest tidal reach in the world".

The alley was as dark as a Scandi thriller, and the two of them were walking arms out in front like zombie extras. Danny kicked over a bucket and Pete hissed "Quiet. We don't want to get ourselves arrested. That new magistrate's a bugger." Danny tittered "I suppose you're related to him." "Him's a her" said the mayor with a palpable tinge of fear in his voice. "I suppose we're related by holy headlock." Apparently, her indoors did get out sometimes.

"Did I hear the word headlock?" The owner of the strange falsetto voice burst out of a door, flooding the alleyway with light. He appeared to be a Red Indian. Not a Native American or a First Nation Citizen, but an unreconstructed, pigmentally challenged Red Injun straight out of the Lone Ranger. He was wearing nothing but a few eagle feathers and a suede nappy held together by a prayer and a safety pin.

"This is Bobby Two Rivers" whispered Pete. "Head of Art and Design".

"Your name rings a bell" said Danny.

"You're thinking of Billy Two Rivers, the giant Canadian wrestler. He was from my tribe". Danny found the man's height unnerving, so he didn't labour the point about the name. "I was probably thinking of a water company" Danny finished lamely.

"Anyway" said Bobby after an awkward silence "no need to whisper. There's three police on duty tonight and they're all in there, losing".

Danny was met with a colourful sight. At one end of a long, thin room were three huddles of humanity. They were indulging in the town's two pastimes: bowling and swearing. One member of the Oxbridge Pigs, still in full uniform, had just released his wooden ball, which rolled promisingly along the warped planks until it veered off course just before the skittles and rolled impotently into the gutter. "Bad luck, sarge" sang a female voice unsympathetically. After a few more similar failed attempts, one of the home team stepped up and released a ball, which wobbled alarmingly all over the track before obliterating the skittles with a satisfying thunk.

"You've got to know your alley" Pete yelled into Danny's ear. "That's why playing on your home track is such a huge advantage. The Swan-uppers haven't lost a match here since 1937, when the thugs from the Cat and Bourgeois went the aerial route. They were banned for life, but not before Grand Malc had sustained his brain injuries. You can still see him doddering around town, living up to his new nickname of the Senile Delinquent".

Danny didn't stay long. Pete asked him to stay for the Officiallies and Danny was intrigued enough to do so. Five minutes later, the landlady popped her head round the corner and bellowed "Time, gentlemen please!" Sergeant Ayres of the Oxbridge Pigs led the traditional response: "Officially!"

Then the landlady shouted "Time, ladies please!", at which the whole Hell's Grannies team yelled back "Officially!"

"I'm afraid He Who Must Be Ignored has forgotten to buy the scotch egg, so we can't pretend to be a restaurant again" explained the hostess. To tumultuous cheering, she proclaimed this to be a lock-in. "Anyone wishing to leave must use the back passage" she added, to much laughter.

Danny shook Pete's hand and waved goodbye to the others. He followed the landlady out of the room. A young priest was their only companion. The three policemen were not going anywhere.

The Stealth Inspector

On his short walk back to the hotel, Danny fumbled in his pocket and found a disturbingly realistic cat's paw. It even felt warm. Attached was a tiny key labelled Persian. He was feeling tired but he still had a speech to write. It had to be on the Señora's desk tomorrow morning before 6.30. Danny was glad about the early start. He didn't want to be seen around the school before the launch on Saturday. It meant that he would miss Chaos Day, which he would have liked to see out of sheer curiosity. Never mind, he thought smugly, I have people for that. He must have said the last bit out loud, because a tramp-like figure was glaring at him from a shop doorway. This just had to be Grand Malc, thought Danny. The town's only senile delinquent spat and shouted "F***ing nutter".

Danny was starting to feel better about the paddle steamer Waverley. She was a beautiful ship. The detail in the wood and glass work was astonishing, and he felt guilty about calling her a gin palace. She was just a palace which happened to sell gin. Nevertheless, he was relieved to see Lundy getting bigger by the minute but they still didn't seem to be heading straight for it. The captain's announcement cleared that up, but not in a way that Danny liked. Apparently, this was the world's only ocean-going paddle steamer and that meant that, from time to time, she had to venture out into the open Atlantic. Today's conditions were good enough for them to attempt a circumnavigation of the island. Danny didn't like the sound of the word "attempt".

Nothing untoward seemed to be happening as they rounded the northern end of the island. They were hugging the granite cliffs. Just within drowning distance, Danny thought. Then it started: the slow stately bronco ride, where the paddles rarely touched the water. Next stop Boston, thought Danny, the grand old US of A, where swell meant something good. He wondered what Mark Twain would have done in this situation. Danny supposed he'd probably have changed his name to Mark Three Thousand.

Now that they were back in the saner waters of the Bristol Channel, Danny's thoughts turned back to his forthcoming speech to the staff of Hartles School. From what he had heard from Uncle Pete and the rest of Team Danny, the Señora's start of term address had done little to pave the way for him. Those who could hear next to none of the Head's speech were almost as confused as the people who heard most of it. Never mind, he thought, that was always just the icing on the windscreen.

Once they were bobbing safely in the tiny harbour, Danny rushed off the boat and promptly fell head first onto the concrete jetty. In a rare moment of self doubt - or maybe it was a case of mild concussion - Danny heard a voice inside his head say "I hope it's me that's got this right and not Grand Malc".

Chapter 7 – Chaos Day

"Today today is the fifth of September

And the chaos is the worst I can remember"

Today today was indeed Chaos Friday, and Phil Rossall would hear this refrain ad several hundred times nauseam. He had been looking forward to this day with a curiosity that would have killed a whole litter of cats, nine lives apiece. He felt the whole school deserved a treat after yesterday's Inaudible Assembly. In fact, he was unfortunate enough to have been sitting near the front, so he caught plenty of the horribly familiar jargon. He was excited about tomorrow's staff outing to Lundy Island, but today it was back to herding cats.

The two-line ear worm was not exactly a triumph of scansion or grammar, Phil thought, but who was he to criticise? He was merely the first "above board" German teacher for a while, whereas the man who dreamed all of this up was a PR genius and a master of child psychology. The man in question, Hartles School's deputy head Uncle Peter Smythe, was leading the dance, taking the whole school's population through every room in the building, not forgetting the huts, outhouses and outdoor space, including the bike shed, where the sixth formers enjoyed their herbal cigarettes. Leaving no turn unstoned, as Uncle Pete put it.

At the head of the eight hundred strong procession danced Uncle Pete himself, if dancing was the right word. He was trying to keep in time with the school brass band's horrendition of the Helston Floral Dance.

This would have been easier if the band had settled on one rhythm themselves. As it was, the deputy head hopped randomly from one foot to the other as if he were running barefoot across a Spanish beach.

Pete was wearing the full regalia of the Hartles Lord of Misrule: white smock, white breeches, knee-length socks, mayoral chain, horn-rim glasses, bells and army surplus webbing. Phil found it a hard look to describe. Provisional wing of the Morris Men, perhaps? Together with his shuffling gait and man-spread stance, he was a sight to strike fear into a New Zealand haka.

Phil thought the procession was the strangest thing he had ever seen. Behind Uncle Peter and the band, complete with backwards walking conductor, came the Sprogs. They were led by the Head of Year One, Daoud al Zafani, known to his friends as Crispy Dave. He was always in charge of the new intake. In Hartles, the pupils and form teachers moved up the school, but the Heads of Year did not. This meant that the specialist pastoral staff had developed their own unique style, based on years of experience of their allotted age group. Dave's style was best described as Pantomime. He started training the children while they were still in primary school, where the staff gave strict instructions to contradict everything their guest said, and to do the opposite of what he told them to do.

"Good morning, children. I am Mr Al from Big School."

"Oh no you're not" came the perfectly synchronised reply.

"You're really going to hate it at Big School."

"Oh no we aren't / won't" came the less slick liturgical response. Never mind, there was plenty of time for practice.

"Now you will go to Hartles School and beat up all the older children."

"Oh no we won't"

It took some of them a little longer than most to catch on, but children are great ones for conformity. The main thing to remember was that pantomime rules only applied to Mr Al.

One thing the children were strictly forbidden to do was to refer to him as Crispy Dave. They knew this because he had expressly told them to do so.

However, he was more than happy to regale new staff with a slice of his personal history. He would look for new colleagues in the pub - in this case Ginny Reeves and Phil Rossall - pull up a chair and say "I suppose you are wondering why someone like me ended up in a backwater like this."

Phil decided to say nothing.

"Well, it was like this" said Daoud Al Zafani, alias Crispy Dave, warming to his task. "I was hounded out of my home by cultural and religious intolerance. And where was that, I hear you ask. God's own country. That's right folks, Yorkshire. Bingley, to be precise. Less cold than Leeds, less shit than Bradford. My home town has lots of followers of Islam. So many that the white racists called the place Bingleydesh. I was one of the muslims, although I am of Middle Eastern extraction, so I prefer Cloudy Arabia."

49

Crispy Dave took a long and much needed breath. His pint disappeared in record time, and Phil went to the bar without being asked. He had never felt so rich in his life. He even had an extra £200 in his bank account, courtesy of a Mr Inky Stephens. He had no idea what he had done to earn the money, or who Inky was, although the name did ring a faint bell.

When Phil returned with the drinks, he found that Crispy Dave had continued the story without him.

"So you can see why I lost weight" Dave ploughed on "and that was my downfall. The occasional work at Binglesnaks was boring, but I needed the money to finance my studies. I only had a few months to go for my PGCE, but I was burning the candle at both ends. One night, I was doing the graveyard shift on the crisp fryer when my ring fell off. It was of great sentimental value, but in recent weeks it had become too big for me. It slipped off into the crisps, so I rolled up my right sleeve and thrust my hand into the vat as soon as the oil had drained away. We had protective gear but no one ever wore it. I managed to get my arm out relatively unscathed, minus some skin - and without the ring, of course."

Dave surfaced again for air and looked longingly at his empty glass. But he was too deep into his story to stop now.

"I thought I could get my arm to safety before the spray came down, but I was too slow. A fine mist of ultra-concentrated flavouring coated the back of my hand and changed my life forever. I was barred from the mosque. Nobody would speak to me. For weeks, the smell lingered" he sobbed.

Phil was baffled, but then Dave looked up and cried "It was only Crispy bloody Bacon flavour!"

Phil suppressed an urge to shout "Oh no it wasn't!" He decided instead to help Dave drown his sorrows.

Phil's enjoyment of Chaos Day was not exactly enhanced by the mother of all hangovers. But at least, as a Fourth Form tutor, he was a long way from the band. Unfortunately, his new form made up for this by singing the two lines of the Hartles Floral Dance incessantly at lung volume 10. The noise generated by his twenty-eight charges was an assault on his eardrums. Fourteen and fifteen-year-olds teemed around him shout-singing in their precocious and pubescent voices. They grow up quick round here, Phil thought. So this was Four Rossall, his brand new tutor group. He wondered how much tutoring would be going on this year.

Ahead of Four Rossall marched years one to three and the rest of the fourth year. The fifth year slouched along behind him, pretending not to enjoy the day. Even the sixth formers joined in, albeit ironically. To misquote Uncle Pete, eight hundred and twenty-three people and children were taking part in this year's slow motion stampede, and heaven help anyone who didn't play their part to the full.

Over lunch in a quiet room next to the canteen, Tio Pepe told Phil the tale of the one and only transgressor in the Chaos Day's fifteen-year history.

"Foolishly" said Pete "the Jefe sat all the kids down in the assembly hall and asked them who had turned on the Bunsen burners on their way through the chemistry lab. As no one spoke up - surprise, surprise - she informed them that the rest of the day was cancelled. They were told to go straight home. The hall was empty before Señora Hartles had finished mumbling."

Pete was starting to get angry, his horn rim glasses steaming up in sympathy. "You know, that's the only time in the last eight years that Bates has ever made himself useful. He may not be much of a PE teacher, but he earned his crust that day."

Phil was intrigued but a little queasy about the deputy head's candour. "Surely he can't be that bad." He meant this to be supportive, but it sounded more like he was fishing.

Pete didn't seem to notice. "You think so?" he whispered vehemently. "If all the male teachers are addressed as Sir or Señor, and your name is Bates, you don't let the kids call you Master."

"But how was Bates useful?" asked Phil, now hopelessly lost.

"He could run fast, couldn't he?" said Uncle Pete, as if he were talking to a toddler.

Pete took pity on him and said "He managed to catch up with the lynch mob before too much damage had been done. He got the rope off the boy's neck and faced down a hundred homicidal children until I could get there."

Phil decided to ask a really stupid question. "Is that why they call it the Hanging Oak?" Pete didn't dignify that with an answer. He continued "It took me days to sort out the bloody fiasco."

Undaunted, Phil said "Is that why you have such a stranglehold on the school and the town? A hundred hushed-up cases of attempted murder must have given you plenty of material for your little tea and blackmail chats."

Uncle Pete did an unintentionally comic double-take. His face clearly betrayed his thoughts. "Maybe this newbie's not the dud I took him for."

Phil risked one more question. "But I still don't understand why we need a Chaos Day. Why do you lead us all such a merry dance every year?" But the mayor had spent long enough on the new German teacher.

"Sorry, Phil, things to see, people to do" he said, already retreating. I suggest you ask any of the old lags. Anyone but Jackanory, that is. And you need to know before you go to Lundy. In other words, tonight. Sicknote will do admirably. She walks her dog in Rockpool Park from 7.32 to 8.28 every evening. She'll set you right if anybody can." And with that, Uncle Pete was gone.

Phil was not sure he liked the implication in Pete's parting shot that he was slow on the uptake. But a little light leg-pulling could not mask the feeling that he was being courted, or perhaps groomed. Not like a pedigree dog and definitely not like a sex-trafficked child, but he still felt like a pawn in someone else's chess game. Phil believed the old adage: you're not paranoid if they really *are* all out to get you. But this seemed more like a charm offensive. Ever since Dartington, he had been asking himself the same question: what's so special about me?

Whatever it was, it certainly wasn't his dancing. During the fifth and final lap, Phil tripped and nearly fell as he was coming out of the library. His tutor group carried on as if nothing had happened, and he had the strange experience of being danced around by a couple of hundred fifth and sixth formers. He was now at the very back. Phil smiled at the two people whose job it was to bring up the rear. Gerry Mee, the other deputy, smiled back, but carried on dictating a string of numbers and letters, like a demented dentist. The dictatee was Phil's predecessor Liesl, the non-German non-teacher. She was carrying a huge clipboard and was furiously writing notes as they shuffled along.

In their handover chat, Liesl had told him about what happened on Chaos Day and what he was required to do. Only now did Phil realise how underprepared he had been. He didn't know what to do next, but at least he seemed to have got away with his little faux pas. He breathed a sigh of relief.

Then the music stopped and he heard the voice of Crispy Dave booming out "Where's Señor Rossall?"

And eight hundred children shouting in unison

"He's behind you!"

Chapter 8 - Little Miss Quickfix

It was a beautiful day for it. Sunshine, good company, relatively flat seas. Phil Rossall felt he had died and gone to Devon, home of the web-footed sparrow and the clotted cow. Everyone was in a good mood, considering they were being asked to work on a Saturday. It didn't feel like work, though. Phil had spent most of the outward journey on deck, basking in the unseasonal sun and tasting the seasoning salt in the wind. He had joined his fellow newcomer, Ginny Reeves, as she watched the giant paddle turn.

"Magnificent, isn't it?" she said to him by way of greeting. "Magnificent and stupid. Whoever thought that was a good way to propel a ship?"

"Not Brunel, for one" Phil replied. "A hundred years before this beautiful anachronism was built, he had rejected paddles in favour of propellers. They said he was mad. Ok, he was a bit of a homicidal maniac, but he was right."

They stood on in silence, taking in the scene. Then Ginny blurted out "Tell me, Phil. You know everything. Who is Lazlo Biro?"

"Hungarian inventor of the ballpoint pen" Phil blurted back, forgetting to contradict her. "Why do you ask?"

Ginny looked like she regretted bringing up the topic, but she was committed to it now. "It's just that . . . " she hesitated "just that . . . "

"He paid £200 into your bank account?" said Phil, the penny finally dropping.

"You really do know everything" squealed Ginny. This time, his modesty was in place. But he looked so down in the mouth that she didn't press him for an explanation. They had plenty of time. She left him leaning on the railing, staring at the sea. She could hear him muttering "Stephens' Ink and the ballpoint pen. Some nom de bloody plume. I wonder what pen name comes next. Bic van Bike?"

But who could be downcast on a day like today? Phil was not in the least concerned about the pen-based punnery, which was, to misquote a topical phrase, pretty darned transparent. And he was also not worried that the Hartles staff might think him stand-offish. He had plenty of time to show them how gregarious he was.

Most of his new colleagues were playing cards in the saloon, and they were oblivious to everything else. Early on in the voyage, Phil had watched a game of euchre and had been offered a seat at the table. The invitation had come from the Head of Fifth Form, Bobby Two Rivers. Phil hadn't spoken to him yet, but he recognised him from school. It would have been hard not to. Six foot eight of spectacularly underdressed redness tended to draw the eye towards it. Phil doubted that the threat of the tomahawk in his belt was ever needed.

Unfortunately, Phil had never heard of euchre. Having watched a couple of rounds, he was none the wiser. He was surprised to hear a couple of German words in there, but that did not encourage him. Memories of a train journey across Germany bubbled to the surface. A group of hospitable grandpas from somewhere near

The Stealth Inspector

Munich had given him a hand of cards and some bizarre and nonsensical instructions on how to play Skat. They then proceeded to play a round, guiding him on what to do next. This appeared to have nothing to do with the rules they had just given him. Every so often, at completely random points in the game, someone would knock on the table and the rest of them would throw their hands up in mock despair. Then everyone would reach for the black bread and schnapps. Although not an unpleasant experience, Phil developed a wariness of machiavellian card games and men who wear lederhosen.

Phil was sure he was being unfair to euchre by comparing it to Skat, but he had politely but firmly declined Bobby's offer.

When he saw Huw Davies, the resident maths genius, turn around in his chair at the other table, Phil thought he was in for more of the same. Huw had already approached him on Thursday about joining the yomping on Lundy. This was very different, though. He leaned back and said "Care to join us for some dirty bridge?"

Phil looked non-plussed. In fact, he hadn't been plussed all morning.

"It's not as exciting as it sounds" Huw explained. Pity, thought Phil, that's setting the bar pretty low. Bates, the PE master, decided to join the conversation. He looked witheringly at Phil's legs and said "He can't play. He hasn't brought any shin pads."

Phil was happier here in the open. He needed time to process all the information he had received. Not about the Inky Stephens thing. It would be a shame to have to return the £200, but other than that, the topic barely scratched his consciousness.

Last night's conversation with Sicknote, however, was a very different matter. Phil needed to get his mind round it in the few minutes he had before they got to Lundy.

Dame Antonia Buller-Strachan was easy to recognise. Phil had spotted a short woman with a crew cut and two incongruous dogs coming out of Rockpool House. He was in position at the park entrance before she even crossed the road.

"Punctual. I like that" she said in clipped Scottish tones. "You are wondering who I am, why you haven't seen me in school yet, why I'm called Sicknote, what these dogs are called and what the hell all that floral dancing was about."

"Er . . . yes" was the best that Phil could do. She had even got the order of the questions right.

She didn't miss a beat. "Army surgical corps, tours of Africa and Asia, then that old oxymoron military intelligence, government fixer . . . " Sicknote paused and looked at Phil. Then she relaxed.

"At MI6, I was known by a letter, not M or Q, of course. I could tell you which, but then I'd have to kill you."

Phil was about to laugh dutifully at the old joke when he risked a quick glance at her face and decided to keep stumm. He still thought it was a joke, but he wasn't taking any chances.

"MI6 was a pretty dull affair. The service was full of fantasists and testosterone cowboys. I was head-hunted by someone in Cabinet Office to join the team, which meant I was working not indirectly but still deniably for the PM. I was paid some obscene salary - under the counter, of course - to ensure my loyalty, because I knew where the bodies were buried. I should do: I had put some of them there myself."

Phil opened his mouth to ask whether this too was a figure of speech, but Dame Sicknote diplomatically answered the question he had actually wanted to ask.

"I know it's odd for an old spook to be so forthcoming. Uncle Pete asked me to, which I thought was interesting. I assume he thought you could be trusted.

I came here frequently for my last job, visiting people other agencies had resettled here. None of the locals paid them a blind bit of notice. You could call them Vladimir Spymaster and they would be safe. I had just decided to take early retirement and was thinking about my future when I discovered it: gene pool churn."

Sicknote said this as if it was the most obvious thing in the world. But Phil was getting the hang of this now. He simply waited for her to explain.

"These isolated communities find it hard to hang on to their cleverest young people, who leave for jobs and the bright lights. Conventional wisdom says that birth rates are not keeping pace with this loss of talent."

"Not even with Jan Ridd around?" Phil asked flippantly.

Sicknote was silent and, just for a moment, her face was like thunder. Eventually, a thin smile returned and she said quietly "My, you are a clever one. Anyway, my Flopsy is a six-month-old, nineteen-stone Newfoundland and Mopsy's the local breed, Jack Russell. She terrierises the poor boy mercilessly, even though she's only a puppy too. They're both still intact. They may eventually want to mate. Tricky logistics, but it would be fun watching them try."

Conscious that he had overstepped the mark, Phil thought it wise to feign an interest in the dogs, even though he was running out of time.

"You have failed to find out how I became school nurse and counsellor." she continued regardless. "The children come to me because I can't be arsed to go into school for anything less than a broken leg. So Pete christened me Sicknote, because I sign off on the kids' absences, while being the biggest skiver of the lot.

The Hartles Floral Dance thing is simple enough. Like so many traditions in this country, it was born out of incompetence and despair. Which is a rather good and long overdue epitaph for Gerry Mee. He was appointed back in the day for the sole purpose of writing the school timetable.

Now, I'm not pretending that writing a school timetable is easy. There are lots of moving parts, or rather there should be. You need to juggle four balls: pupils, teachers, location and time. Gerry was OK with the balls but not so good at the juggling.

He could have done some research before he started. Maybe studied last year's timetable, talked to a few colleagues. But no, Gerry rocked up two weeks before the start of the school year, locked himself in his office and emerged, smelly but triumphant, on D-day Minus One.

At the pre-term briefing, Gerry presented his meticulously colour-coded timetable to the staff, who were understandably anxious to know who they would be teaching next year, not to mention tomorrow. Gerry's smart handout packs gave them all an individual plan for each day, itemising every mortal detail of their new charges. Pete told me you could hear a pin drop as people checked their free periods and who they would be teaching last thing on a Friday."

"But . . . " said Phil hesitantly.

"But indeed" Sicknote told the whole park. "Give that man a doggy chew! Gerry had answered the who, what and when, but had forgotten about the where. Apparently, you're supposed to start your new timetable with the rooms, or the specialist locations at least. That is, if you don't want to teach swimming in the library or fifth year chemistry on the football pitch.

This was all before my time here, but I can feel the trauma around the place. When the fiasco was discovered, it was too late to do anything about it. They had a timetabler who couldn't organise a cock-up in a hen house, and the kids were coming in at nine the next morning.

As it happened, it turned out much worse than they had feared. Jostling, barging, running around like headless chickens. And that was just the staff. The children went full throttle berserk. Over a hundred of them tried to get into room 12A at once. It was discovered to have a partial view of the games changing rooms. By half past nine, the school was heading for nuclear reactor meltdown. And then the fire alarm went off, trumping the kids' noise and soaking them with the sprinklers.

Years of fire drill practice kicked in and, like the good Pavlovian dogs that they were, they made their way to the field, where Uncle Pete greeted them with a beatific smile. The prefects were on hand to usher them calmly to their tutor group area, where they lined up in alphabetical order. They were soon joined by their equally bedraggled form teachers, who took the soggy register and then got their charges to sit quietly and wait. The sproglets made a beeline for Mr Al, alias Crispy Dave, who told them precisely what not to do. The rest of the day was cancelled.

Uncle Pete told the staff what was going to happen the next day, and then he went off to practise with the band. On his way home, he stopped at the bookie's.

The brass band repertoire was the Cornish Floral Dance. That was it. Not very Oxbridge, but at least Pete was spared the agony of choice."

She glanced at her watch and said "The rest you know. You were dancing through Gerry Mee's beautifully constructed, incomplete timetable. What you won't have noticed was that, at every break in the music, class representatives sloped off to the gym to hand to the Head Girl and Boy their betting slips on which they had scrawled the number of their desired room."

Sicknote paused and smiled fondly. "It's crazy. It's a cross between Ascot and Argos. It has no right to work. But it does, every time."

Phil was jolted out of his reverie by the noise of the ship's gangway crashing into place. Suddenly, he was in a rush to get off the Waverley. He joined the short line and was soon setting foot on Lundy Island. There seemed to be some sort of commotion ahead of him, and he saw a figure sprawled out in front of him. Phil offered the man a helping hand, smiled in his face and said "Hello Ducky."

Chapter 9 - The sermon on the rock

It was nine months since Professor Danny Duckworth had attended that inaugural Ofsted meeting, and he was more than ready to give birth. He was relishing his role as the Office for Standards in Education's very own Glitch-finder General. However, he wasn't all that keen on the title his government minder Alec Pryke had jokingly given him. Danny felt it trivialised the role he had carved out for himself. He preferred to be called the Stealth Inspector.

Danny knew full well that he was on an ego trip and travelling First Class. In his mind, he envisioned himself as a pioneer, "driving up" educational standards and "delivering transparency" to schools and parents. Just occasionally, he saw himself as a pompous prat, but not often enough to do anything about it. Most of all, he was absurdly proud of the monitoring and quality assurance systems he had set up to keep Ofsted inspections on the straight and narrow. He was not fazed by the fact that his two undergrad whizz-kids Stuart and Zara had done most of the practical work. That's why Danny called it practical work: he had practically nothing to do with it. He was a great one for infrastructure, as long as someone else was digging the ditches.

That suited the rest of Team Danny just fine. Zara was happy to follow family tradition and stay in the murky background. She still couldn't believe that anyone was willing to pay her for doing a couple of hours of mental gymnastics a week. It was more interesting than her History course, which she could do standing on her head. Stuart was always happy to stay out of the limelight. He was flourishing in his PPE studies, and had fallen in love with Economics. It was something you could do in a darkened room, well away from other people. Quite how this tallied with his new look was a mystery, not least to Stuart himself. He was celebrating his Scottish roots by covering his body, such as it was, in garish, clashing tartan. Mercifully, he had stopped short of wearing a kilt, but the tartan trousers made him look like Rupert Bear channelling his inner Braveheart.

Stuart's original schools spreadsheet had evolved into what he called a multidimensional database. In addition to the general information on every school in the country, it now held every mortal detail from the first fifteen Ofsted inspections carried out since that fateful meeting nine short months earlier.

The plan was to test out the assessment regime devised by the **SPY** working group in advance of the public launch. At least, that was *their* plan. Their political masters had different ideas. Danny woke up one morning to the sound of his alarm radio blaring on about "failing schools". The government had published the first fifteen inspection reports in full and issued a press release proclaiming that Leafy Suburban Grammar was performing outstandingly well and Grotbag Sink Estate Comprehensive was doing unacceptably badly.

Most galling for Danny and his colleagues on the SATAN working group was that they had no prior warning of this debacle, whereas the hounds of Fleet Street had obviously been fed the tastiest morsels well in advance. The story was all over the front pages like a rash, and the focus was on failing schools. The Times and the Telegraph led with pseudo thoughtful pieces on how the youth of today was going to hell in a handbasket. The Mail and the Express were full of shouty headlines and invective about do-good liberals and the abandonment of traditional British values. One particularly disreputable article by Penny Junor was full of unattributable anecdotes on how Grotbag Comprehensive had lost control of its pupils. It was accompanied by a full-page photo of a nose-ringed girl throwing up in a hedge.

Team Danny had only just started analysing the results from the first wave of pilot inspections. Not all the data were in yet. One of the sixteen planned reports had so far failed to materialise. All Danny had received from this group was a tissue of insultingly thin excuses. This was not the type of transparency Danny was looking for. No, Dr Patten, the dog did not eat your report, nor did you leave it on a bus. Just for a few minutes, Danny wondered whether all this evidence gathering was actually worthwhile. National government, the press and probably a good chunk of the general public had already made up their minds about the quality of English education. Any evidence from Ofsted would be used selectively to bolster up their existing prejudices. Danny didn't know whether to be peeved or miffed, so in the end he settled for pissed off.

But the opportunity to get his hands on some privileged data and analyse the hell out of it was too good to pass up. Team Danny was on the hunt for anomalies again, but these would be very different from the ones that led them to Hartles School, Oxbridlesturridge. If all went to plan, however, the results of this new search should take them straight back to the kingdom of Uncle Pete.

What Danny and his minions were after were schools in the first batch of fifteen inspections that had much better or much worse results than expected. That was easy to say but hard to prove. And excessively dull to explain. Danny felt he could bore for England on the subject but, in reality, he wasn't even that interesting. Stuart knew his stuff, but he never ventured out from the safety of jargon.

Zara listened to their stream of drivel and said "So you take a bunch of surveys and score our fifteen schools on the quality of their education, using a scale based on the Ofsted criteria. Then you compare the scores with their actual inspection results and look for our old friend Mr Anomaly."

"Well, yes" said Danny, looking a little disappointed. "But we have unprecedented access to unpublished data. The index we have constructed gives us another way of evaluating schools. We can map it against the Ofsted scores and look for outliers."

"Oh, I remember the outlier" chirped Zara. "Apart from being a spectacularly low scorer at Scrabble, it's an indication of shouldn't-be-there-ness."

In fact, even the small set of fifteen schools had yielded three cases worthy of another look. But when Dr Patten's report winged its grudging way to Ofsted Towers, Danny realised they were in a whole new ballgame. Danny snapped up the data and delivered them to his statistician's waiting tartan arms. The written report could wait, but he did note that the master copy looked well chewed.

It didn't take long to fit Penny Hassle School, Wiltshire into Team Danny's database. The sixteenth report completed the first round of inspections. Within a couple of hours, Stuart was singing a Robbie Burns song, complete with modal tune and a noise reminiscent of two cats falling off a cliff, which was Stuart's version of the bagpipes. Danny couldn't stop himself looking over Stuart's shoulder, chuckling softly to himself, while Zara fixed one of her family's trademark cocktails, which she had renamed the Penny Hassle. While sipping contentedly, the team looked at the charts Stuart had produced. He had to change the scale to fit the new results in. Any more of an outlier and Penny Hassle School would be in orbit.

"How on earth did such a god-awful school get inspection scores like that?" Stuart enquired of no one in particular.

"Pure comedy gold" observed Zara, raising her glass.

"Next stop Oxbridlesturridge" said Danny.

In fact, the next important stop was Lundy. As soon as that annoying Phil Rossall had helped him to his feet and stopped gloating, Danny was keen to get going. "Inky Stephens, I presume" indeed! It was funny how people could shrink on you. But, when he did start climbing the steep path towards the island's central plateau, progress was by no means easy. First came the two -way traffic. The entire population of Lundy Island seemed to be tramping down towards the harbour. This was because it was. Currently, there were thirty people living on the rock, and they were all eager to board the Waverley for their free food and drink. When the traffic jam had cleared, Danny started to enjoy the climb and the sea air. Suddenly, a galumphing sound enveloped him from behind and a yokel in ill-fitting wellingtons passed him at speed, pursued by three men in hiking gear muttering something that sounded like "yomp, yomp, yomp".

The sign stuck to the front door of the pub couldn't have been clearer:

"Hartless Party, help yourself to whatever you want. Ploughmen in the kitchen."

Despite the generosity of this offer, Danny Duckworth sensed the undertone of excitement in the handful of residents and visitors who had rushed onto the Waverley. Although they didn't stop to chat, they gave the strong impression that they had the better side of the deal. An afternoon booze cruise and buffet lunch was too good to pass up. Natural beauty and solitude were all very well, but a little luxury would do no harm.

Fortunately, the school party felt the same way. They had three hours to take in the wild beauty of the island before they were to be back at the pub for a late lunch. Most colleagues chose to amble down to the lighthouse at the far end of the island to admire the cliffs and look for birdlife. When they got there, they found the four yompers stretched out in the sunshine. They seemed happy enough, despite their complaints that the terrain was too easy.

"Been right round the island, and there's barely a tussock worthy of the name" Bobby Chudleigh announced to all and sundry. "And you won't find any puffins. They buggered off to Greencliff six months ago."

A healthy happy group of teachers congregated in the pub. The ploughmen had done their work, and the unlimited beer and wine was having the desired effect. So when Uncle Pete got to his feet, there was a contented hush.

"As you know" said Pete "I am not one for giving speeches . . ." This was greeted with gales of mirth from every corner of the crowded pub.

"First, I would like to ask the Head to say a few words. The Head did, probably.

When Señora Hartles had sat down - seemingly in the middle of a sentence, but no one was complaining - Pete passed the baton to the other deputy Gerry Mee. Apart from being quite tall, Gerry was notable as a sporting failure. The football team for whom he was the third choice goalkeeper had miraculously reached the final of the FA Cup. This was appropriate for Gerry, who had FA to do with it. But during their run to the Final, the minnows had lost their goalkeeper to serious injury. His understudy played a big part in his team's win in the semifinal, but got himself sent off for punching his own centre half. The referee looked rather embarrassed as he pointed towards the dressing room, but he was quite right. Ironically, the centre half took over the goalie's jersey, and fumbled his way to victory.

Once the euphoria had died down, the manager realised he had a problem. His pugilistic goalkeeper was banned from his next Cup match, and that was the Final. Gerry was going to get his first team debut in the biggest game in his club's history. He picked up the nearest thing to hand - a heavy cut glass fruit bowl - to mime lifting the trophy, but the bowl slipped from his hands and buried itself in his left foot. Butterfingers Mee watched the game from his hospital bed and never played again.

Gerry's aptitude for snatching defeat from the jaws of victory had not deserted him. He talked the staff through what he called the iterative timetable and told them what to do in the likely event that it broke down. Uncle Pete thanked his colleague and said he was glad the timetable was in safe hands. When the chuckling had stopped, he continued "Some of you may have seen the gentleman to my right around town recently. This is Professor Danny Duckworth, one of the country's leading teacher trainers."

Now it was Danny's chance to make his pitch. Pete had advised him to avoid pomposity and educational jargon, which Danny addressed by failing on both counts in his very first sentence. Nevertheless, they liked the sound of Danny's proposal.

"I'm making a short film for trainee teachers" he said, "and I want to show them what life is like in a school such as yours."

That sounded enough like a compliment to keep everyone listening.

"It would be what they call a fly on the wall documentary. The cameras follow you around so much, you forget they are there."

"Will we be famous?" someone asked.

"I doubt it" replied Danny "although you will be seen by thousands of young students aspiring to join the profession. It's intended to stimulate lively debate."

That got a laugh, but a gentle and inclusive one.

"Jackanory could tell them one of his wartime stories".

Danny didn't know why that was funny, but he laughed along with everyone else. "Although" he lied, going in for the kill "there's a production company called Parker and Schaefer, who are interested in the idea of a series of school documentaries called Bringing Up. So this could act as a pilot. In the future, we may see a series on the telly, and the first one would be Bringing Up Oxbridge."

Uncle Pete was keen to wind things up, so he asked "What do the staff have to do?"

"Just ignore the cameras and teach" said Danny.

"So who'll be playing me?" asked Bates.

A crisp Yorkshire voice answered from the gloom at the back "That's a tricky one. Stan Laurel is dead."

Chapter 10 - Cameras roll

The camera crew looked very familiar, especially to some of the children who lived in the rural areas around and about. Some were even related, which was hardly surprising, given the empire-building fecundity of the Ridds of Ridd Mires. Some of the teachers recognised them too. They were the sons of Caleb Ridd, who was in turn one of the adult offspring of Jan and Martha Ridd. Jan had divorced Martha years ago, but she still lived with Jan and his exploded family, and she frequently forgot that they were no longer married. Jan often seemed quite forgetful too.

Rick and Mick were in their early twenties and were known as the Twins, which seemed biologically unlikely, as Mick was white and Rick was black. They were two of the better earners in the extended household, because they did the filming for Jan's burgeoning porn production company. It would be a challenge for them to shoot scenes in which the people were not horizontal, but Jan was paying them well. Anyway, they were at a bit of a loose end until work started on the next film, Lorna Goes Doone.

It seemed odd not to have Grandpa Jan calling all the shots, but his instructions had been clear: film whatever you want, and we'll worry about the editing later. As Old Hartlesians of the rural kind, Rick and

Mick knew exactly where to start. There were six buses which took about 250 children to Hartles School from the outlying areas. A couple fetched them from the South, where the milkmaids wore headscarves to distinguish them from the cows. Another two ventured into the Deep West, where men were men and sheep were nervous. The remaining buses covered the eastern part of the school's huge catchment area. But none went as far as Rocky's Coaches, which drove all the way out to White Witch Rocks. There was nobody mad or brave enough to live out by the Rocks except for the multigenerational family of William "Rocky" Rollworthy. The farm was run down and messy. There were rumours of an impending curse, though it was hard to see what damage a curse could do. But Rocky loved it out here. Agriculture would never generate a living for the family. They lived off potatoes and the occasional lamb. Then Rocky's granddaughter turned eleven and had to go to the "nearest" secondary school in Oxbridge. So he did what any self-respecting Exmoor Mudraker would do. He carried his chainsaw and his welding gear over to the farm's vehicle graveyard, selected the wreck that most closely resembled a bus and Frankensteined the hell out of it. Then he massively undercut the existing service provider, and Rocky's Coaches was born. The use of the plural wasn't strictly accurate, as Rocky's was a fleet of one, but this bus was a true hybrid. There were forty usable seats, behind which was a tangle of sharp rusty shards. The engine came from an era when smoke was a good thing. There was no suspension and the brakes were prayer assisted.

Rick and Mick were in position at the top end of Mires Lane by 8am, camera and sound boom at the ready. Rick had asked Rocky for permission to film on board the Hartles express, which he was happy to give if they helped to promote his tours for holiday makers. They planned to film the bus arriving and focus on the side where a shoddily hand painted sign read "Ride Rocky's, where every tour is a mystery".

For the children from the remote farms like Ridd Mires, travelling by school bus constituted a major time investment. Over the course of a week, they would spend about five hours learning Maths and up to seven hours staring at Gaffer Rocky's bald patch.

The dumplings did indeed spend most of the journey time looking vacantly into space, oblivious of the spectacular scenery passing by the mud-spattered windows. Scrogg, a fourteen year old wannabe thug, was fond of aping his father's catchphrase "You can't eat the view", to which the standard response was "You ever heard of tourists?". But there were relatively few dumplings on board Rocky's Rocket. If you wanted the full dumpling experience, you needed to ride the southern bus with the Zombies of Holthamleigh.

The Stealth Inspector

The bus-kids also missed out on after school and weekend activities, so they could never join the splendidly attritional rugby team, whose aim was to keep the ball hidden for the entire match. But there were consolations for the kids on the slow lanes. Rick and Mick remembered them from their own years in captivity, and they were eager to film them. But things had changed since the advent of the Ridd Sextuplets. They were just starting their third year of secondary education, and it was still unclear whether they or Hartles School were on the steeper learning curve.

Rick and Mick Ridd certainly came from a complicated family, and they weren't very good at genealogy. They felt like twins, they shared a birthday and a brain. But they could not explain why they looked so different from each other. Rick's suggestion that Mick was an albino version of himself was greeted with universal derision. Grandpa Jan was no help. He knew he was the father, but could remember nothing about the mother or mothers. The position of the sextuplets in the Ridd family forest was more straightforward. Anyone observing Mother Earth's transition from curvy to beachball could have no doubts about their maternity. As the six were the sons of their grandfather, Rick reckoned they were his uncles, or possibly half-uncles, if such a thing existed.

One advantage of being a bus-kid was that you never had to worry about homework. They had been organised into work groups by 5 Ridd, who was the entrepreneur of the Sixers. 5 was happy to let Rick and Mick film the homework groups in action. They got some nice footage of the younger kids helping each other and of the older rocketeers helping the little ones. The system 5 had set up even catered for the sixth formers who had a problem with their own work. It didn't happen very often, so Rick and Mick jumped into action as soon as they heard the sing-song call "Hey Moll". Molly Stidworth made her way to the back of the habitable parts of the bus, closely followed by the camera crew. First impressions would have cast her as a typical dumpling: fair hair, stout build, low brow. All that was missing were the headscarf and milking stool. But when she started speaking, everything changed. She settled on the lap of the nearest sixth former, in this case belonging to Beth from Dullerton.

The film makers couldn't believe their luck as they captured Molly's virtuoso performance. She listened to the description of the problem, which could be anything from Newton's second law of motion to French subjunctives. In this case, an upper sixth former they called Hair-gel Tony was stuck on a question about the formation of glacial valleys.

"I dunno" Molly said "I'm only fifteen. A level Geography, that's that vindictive sod Hall, isn't it? Ok, you be Hall and I'll be you" she ordered, miming rubbing something into her hair. "Ask me some horrible questions."

Molly did a comic impression of Tony slumped over his desk, bored out of his tiny mind, while the real Tony really got into his role, firing questions at the class. As soon as he had finished the seventh question, Molly's hand shot up and she shouted "Please Señor Hall Sir, what is the answer to that?" As soon as Tony started to formulate Hall's reply, the audience could almost hear the penny drop. They laughed at his vacant expression as he experienced his lightbulb moment. Molly got up, kissed him on the forehead and danced her way to the front of the bus.

"Got the whole thing, including the money shot" said Mick.

"Yeah" replied Rick. "That's a wrap. We'll get the card schools on the way home."

Rick and Mick still couldn't believe that the school had given them permission to film wherever and whatever they wanted. Did the Head have a death wish? They thought the school didn't have a big problem with discipline, even compared to other schools in the area. The twins had friends who had been in the Siege of Bartlesford, when a crowd of third years had gone on the rampage. That was never going to happen in Hartles, where even the "lynching" had been a practical joke. It had its share of naughty children - and half-uncle 2 was a Grade

A psychopath - but Rick thought that any competent teacher would find Hartles a pretty easy gig. Pity there were so many crap ones.

The twins decided to start by following one of the dud teachers through a typical morning. That should yield a fair amount of photogenic mayhem. They decided that Mr Statham would get them off to a flying start. Abraham Statham was a true Comprehensive teacher. He had comprehensively failed generations of Hartlesians.

The twins were nearly at the door of the Art room, where Mr Statham was supposed to be registering his third-year tutor group. They saw Miss Battleship steaming towards them on intercept course, so they thought it was wise to wait for her broadside where they stood. Neither of them could remember her real name. They had successfully banished her memory but now it suddenly all came back like yesterday's pizza. And she was smiling! Only then did they notice the funny grey man bobbing around in her wake. "Good morning, Ridd and Ridd" she foghorned. Rick wondered telepathically how she would address the sextuplets. Mick sniggered, which earned a stare from Battleship. "I wanted to introduce you to Mr Penman" she said, gesticulating in the direction of Professor Danny Duckworth. "It is he who commissioned the film Bringing Up Oxbridge from your grandfather, who, I believe, makes educational films. I don't know the ins and outs of it."

"Don't worry, Miss. we do" said Rick, failing to keep a straight face.

Battleship looked a little confused, as she sailed off towards her office.

"Not exactly subtle" Danny whispered.

"I seen you up the Mires with grandpa and Uncle Pete. You weren't Mr Penman then" said Mick. "I remember grandpa calling you Professor Duckworth, 'cos it sounded like a character in one of our films."

"Well, here I'm Mr Penman" Danny replied, visibly flustered. "Now get on with it."

That earned him an eye roll from the twins, who started filming before they entered the Art room. It was reading registration today for the third years, but there was precious little evidence of either reading or registering going on. Everyone in the class had a book open, behind which they were either chatting noisily or copying homework. When the camera crew came in, everyone in the class did what Uncle Pete had told them to do: they behaved as if the cameras weren't there. Except for Tourette's Steve of course, who shouted out "Hey look, it's the Porno Twins", which earned him a kick in the shins from each of his neighbours. Mick ignored him and continued to pan across the class, paying particular attention to the girl holding her book upside down.

Rick had only just set up the second camera at the back of the room when Statham came out of the back office, clutching his mug of tea. One of the swot girls came up to his desk and asked if she could take the register back to the office.

"In a minute, girl" he said. Statham was starting his third year with this tutor group, and he hadn't learned their names yet. "I haven't filled it in this morning." For the first time, he looked around the room and saw the cameras. He ignored them and shouted out "Is everyone here?"

"I'm not" came a voice from the back.

"Everyone's here except Lenny Moss" said the nameless swot girl. "I think he might've left."

Statham ticked the register, which was already three dimensional with Tippex. The bell went and the class left the room noisily, with much scraping of chairs and swirling of sweet wrappers.

It was only a matter of seconds before the next group of third years barged in. Despite their unruly entrance, this was a very different group from Statham's own form. Rick and Mick's eyes met from across the room as they mentally high fived each other. These were mainly Townies, and in their midst was the diminutive figure of Bird. She may have been tiny, but if she asked you to do something, you did it, because she was the girlfriend of 2 Ridd. The last person to disappoint her was still in traction.

The Stealth Inspector

Bird winked at the camera as she made her way to the teacher's desk. "Please Señor, we finished our project on trees last week" she lied. "We're doing a module on male reproduction in Human Biology, and we thought it would be great to explore it from an artistic . . . thingumijig" she trailed off lamely.

This was news to the class, who weren't even doing Human Biology this year. But they thought they knew where this was going and listened with baited breath. The cameramen were doing their best to hide their grins. They needn't have bothered. Statham had not been listening. As Bird continued her monologue, he caught the odd phrase like "three tables of pottery and three of drawing." He definitely heard the promise that the class would clean up before break time.

"Come, Señor. Take a seat in the back office. There's antiques on BBC 1."

Bird came back to muted cheers. The class was waiting, modelling clay and pencils at the ready. Bird spread her arms and said "It's Monday, it's 10am, it's cock and balls time. Not you, Paul Bown. You come out here."

Paul took a lot of not-so-gentle persuasion, but eventually he was standing at the front, towering over Bird and casting nervous glances at the class and the cameras.

"I won't do it" he sobbed "and you can't make me."

Bird smiled sympathetically and patted his arm. "Of course I can't make you" she said quietly "but if you don't, I'll be very disappointed."

Paul's shoulders slumped in defeat as he pulled down his zip.

"Bingo" thought Mick.

"Too right, bro" thought Rick. "Bit of a busman's holiday."

Chapter 11 - Ladies who lunch

Rick and Mick were like kids in a sweet shop, which was ironic, because they were filming in the playground by the tuck shop. Children were waiting stoically for their turn at the little window, where Mr Brend was selling chocolate and assorted confectionery. As usual, it was raining, as if this sodden corner of the land was stuck in God's rinse cycle. Noah would have loved it here, thought Rick. Oh well, whatever floats your boat.

Based on the hazy memories of their own time in Hartles, the twins had decided to follow Señor Brend from the tuck shop and into his next lesson which was, according to Mr Mee's timetable, version 9b, first year History. In the meantime, they got some good shots of kids running around in the pouring rain. A group of girls were playing Squash the Frog and a gaggle of boys were immersed in a game of air football. Only a trained eye such as Mick's would have spotted the mischief going down by the side of the tuck shop. Five third year boys wearing rugby shirts were standing round a deep puddle, while a sixth brother held a plastic bag open. The rugby shirts were a rather desperate tactic employed by their head of year to keep tabs on which sextuplet was which. Each of them had their number, or rather their name, sewn onto the back of the shirt. They swapped shirts on average

85

three times a day. The boy with the number 4 shirt, who was actually number 3, was collecting protection money in the form of chocolate. Some of the children, who had been queuing in the rain for their turn at the tuck shop window, were only in possession of their break-time treat for a few seconds. Anyone not cooperating was invited to take a seat in the deep puddle.

Hut D was a hot, steaming mass of humanity. Perry Brend said he was used to a tropical climate from his time in the army. In addition to the first form History class, the back corner of the room was incongruously occupied by fifteen-year-old Molly Stidworth, resplendent in school uniform three sizes too small for her. In two of the other corners were Rick and Mick, cameras already rolling. Brend ignored Molly but glared at the cameras. He reserved a particularly unfriendly stare for Rick, who had helped make Brend's probationary year such a nightmare. Now in his mid thirties, he saw himself as master of his own classroom, and he made it clear that the twins were not welcome.

Mr Brend certainly held the attention of his class and the extras. Molly had decided to come in one of her sixth form free periods to keep an eye on her brother Terrible Terry. She was sitting right behind him. They were "doing" World War 2, as per syllabus, and Brend's summary was pretty unequivocal. It boiled down to: Churchill good, Hitler bad. The Sprogs loved this kind of stuff. It was simple and clear cut, a welcome change for most of them from the shambles of primary school. Molly sat back and took out her knitting. Everyone in the room was waiting for something. In the meantime, they listened politely to their teacher. He told them about Japan entering the war and about the Japanese occupation of south east Asia. He wanted to help these children understand how the presence of the Japanese armed forces affected the lives of people in the region. So he said he would tell them a story from his time in the war. You could hear a pin drop. Even Molly's knitting needles stopped clacking, as Mr Brend told them of the terrible hardships of the Siege of Singapore. He said he was forced to eat rats after the food ran out. He told them about his part in a daring midnight raid behind enemy lines and being so close to a Japanese guard that he could smell the garlic on his breath. He told them how he stopped a military vehicle by lying under it and holding onto the axle with his bare hands.

A much smaller hand was raised and Terrible Terry squeaked "Sir, please Sir. How old were you then?"

Perry Brend looked slightly uncomfortable as he said "Well, I was already a Captain by then, so mid twenties, I suppose."

"Shouldn't you be retired by now?" Terry asked the relatively young teacher. Some of his classmates turned round to give the boy an angry stare. Behind him, his big sister seemed once again engrossed in her knitting.

Then he went too far. "Please sir, is that why they call you Jackanory?"

An icy silence ensued as everyone looked at Mr Brend to see what he would do. Within a split second, there was an almighty "Thwock!" from the back of the room, which echoed around the tiny hut. Only when the noise had died down could they hear the sobbing and groaning coming from the back corner. Terrible Terry had covered his beetroot red face with his fingers, which did nothing to stem the flow of hot, salty water. Behind him, his sister was sitting back, absorbed by her knitting.

"Gotcha" thought Mick "Good job I was ready and waiting. That girl can really shift."

"Yeah" Rick thought back "Sex and violence. And all before lunchtime."

The twins agreed that filming had gone really well that morning. They felt they deserved to take the fourth period off, so that they would be ready to do justice to feeding time at the zoo. Their day job required the camera crew to have a certain level of physical dexterity, but the pace of filming was usually slow. This was mostly because of what Grandpa Jan called "the general question of who-puts-what-where". Then there were the long pauses, while the next lot of little blue pills kicked in. They loved their job, and the money that went with it. But

The Stealth Inspector

Rick just wished that, for once, the plumber would actually fix the bloody leak.

Uncle Pete had told them to use the library office as their base. The library was scarcely used, unless a class found itself temporarily homeless. The office was, not surprisingly, the domain of the librarian, but this was rather a moot point, since she had gone awol on the Spanish town twinning trip two years earlier. Officially, she was still listed as missing, but the signs were not good. On the way home, they had taken the usual ferry line from Santander to Plymouth. The Bay of Biscay was being its usual boisterous self, and the librarian said she was just going out on deck for some air. Presumably, she got too much air, followed by far too much water.

The twins were checking the fruits of their morning's labour, and giggling with glee at some of the more embarrassing bits, when Danny Duckworth's alter ego, Mr Penman, walked straight into the office without knocking. Remind me to dislike that man, thought Rick.

Mick smiled and said "Hello Professor", just to wind him up.

"It's all right if I see some of the footage, isn't it?"

"Quite right" Rick replied "it isn't." The professor may have commissioned the film in the first place, but the twins took their orders from Grandpa Jan and nobody else.

"OK" said Danny, as if it was not OK at all. "I brought you a miniature roving mike, in case you wanted audio from somewhere you can't film."

"Thanks, Prof" they said together, smiling maliciously.

On the way over to the canteen, the camera crew heard what sounded like a whole class chanting swear words in unison. Rick looked up the lesson on the timetable: second year German with Mr Rossall. He had never heard of Mr Rossall, and he had never studied German in his days in Hartles. The subject had not been on his radar until now. He saw on the timetable that the same teacher had a parallel second year German class period 8. The graveyard shift, when the zombies come out of the woodwork.

"You may have to do that one without me" said Mick out loud, which in itself betrayed a slight nervousness.

"Better stick to silent mode, at least until we know exactly what's going on" thought Rick. Mick agreed.

The canteen and most of the kitchen staff hadn't changed in the ten years since the twins were released, but the manager certainly had. Rick could have sworn he had seen her typing away in the school office as he waited at Reception. She wasn't someone you would easily forget. Her appearance was not so much striking as GBH. Her silvery satin cocktail dress had seemed out of place in the office, but in the school cafeteria, it somehow fitted in. This strange woman appeared to be the same shape standing up as sitting down. Rick thought "Oxo cube" and Mick tried to keep a straight face.

"Dahlings" cried the cube "you must be Dick and Ben the video men. And I must be Liesl. Here is Café Hartles and you are welcome to it. Ask of my Ladies That Lunch anything you desire. You are in luck. Today is Wienerschnitzel day."

The twins parked their equipment and went to the counter. The only face they recognised belonged to Mother Inferior, whose proper name - Sister Maria of the Holy Miracle - was not her proper name either. The twins had thought her ancient when they had started big school. They had also called her Scary Mary, Rick remembered fondly, face like a slapped arse and a heart of gold. If you were down in the dumps, she would always give you an extra dollop of mash and a smear of marge. According to the Hartles rumour mill, Mother Inferior used to be Father Brian.

"It's shitsels today, I'm afraid" she said. "Liesl makes us do it. Fried cardboard rolled in sawdust. I'll give you more mash".

"So you don't do the sausage cycle any more?" asked Rick.

"Oh yes. Tuesday to Thursday. Fish fingers on Friday, like it says in the Good Book."

She crossed herself as she handed them the plates. Rick had forgotten that this place was virtually a veg-free zone. Mick also couldn't remember what the sausage cycle was. Must be some sort of bike, he thought. Rick sighed. This telepathy lark was great, except when they were on the toilet, when transmission was mercifully suspended. But it could also be hard work if your partner has the mental capacity of a brain-dead flea.

Rick liked to see himself as an expert on the rural world around him, but he was not as lane-wise as he thought. He knew nothing of the true majesty of the sausage cycle. Basically, it worked like this. The canteen manager and an assistant - in this case, Liesl and Steroid Doris - take the school minibus for a Sunday afternoon drive south into Mid Devon cowboy country. Liesl buys an infeasible amount of pre-condemned stewing steak from Purdew Antiques and Abattoir. The two of them return to their canteen and stew the lot in four vast pots for so long that no bacteria can possibly survive. The stew is served on the Tuesday, and it is so good that there's enough left over to fuel Wednesday's cottage pie and Thursday's sausages. If times were hard, toad in the hole might make a guest appearance on a Friday. Tales of sausage casserole Mondays were largely unfounded.

The twins weren't expecting anything exciting to happen in the canteen. There were too many teachers around. And the presence of a nonagenarian nun at one end of the room and Uncle Pete at the other meant that mischief making was out of the question. The twins got a few minutes of film for local colour, but they also managed to capture the extraordinary spectacle of half a dozen fourth year boys clicking their heels and air-kissing Liesl's hand.

Mick refused to take his camera with him to Hut F. This was the home of the Effers Club and the domain of Rob Burley, alias Mop Bucket. He told Mick that the twins were welcome to film the next day. And then the telepathy stopped. Mick had gone into toilet mode.

Rick suddenly felt tired and lonely. He headed back to the library office to lock away the cameras. Then he saw the tiny microphone on the table. For the first time he saw the remote control receiver and recorder. Tucked underneath was a beautifully hand written note. But it wasn't the calligraphy that made Rick jump for joy, shouting "Nice one, Prof baby!" He checked that there was no one around, but the library was deserted.

For Rick, it was a dream come true. He waited impatiently for afternoon lessons to start, before he went into the corridor. He was so keyed up that he hardly even noticed another class swearing like a Plymouth trawlerman. He walked on, muttering under his breath "Don't knock on the staff room door. Whatever you do, don't knock."

He got to the door.

He knocked.

Chapter 12 - Bad language

It might not be a big deal to everyone, but to Rick Ridd, just knocking on the staff room door felt like breaking a lifelong taboo. It was probably the number one rule in his time at Hartles: "Thou shalt not rattle the teachers' door". The next step suddenly became easier, though no less delicious. Feeling bold as brass, he opened the door and walked in. Not for a second did he feel foolish for having such thoughts, even though he had left school over a decade ago. The twenty-six-year-old Rick felt just as much in awe of this room as he had done when he was eleven. This struck him as odd, because he did not feel the same way about the teachers themselves, with the exception of Uncle Pete and possibly Mop Bucket. But he had to admit that, even now, his reaction to them could not exactly be described as grown-up. The malicious glee with which he was dissecting his old school suddenly started to worry him.

It was not as if he harboured a grudge against Hartles. He did not see himself as a victim of racial prejudice at school. He had been the only black face in a sea of white, but so what? Rick believed that hate was born of fear, and he had been a threat to no one. His fellow pupils did indeed bombard him with insults, but he got no more than everyone else. It never occurred to him that the colour of his skin was a problem, even though he never got away with anything dodgy, because he would always be recognised. But he thought he was simply unlucky to be so easy to spot. Compared to his white twin brother with his learning difficulties, Rick had always had it easy.

He may not have had much of a chip on his shoulder, but Rick was still up for a bit of mischief. He was relieved to find the staff room empty. Since the smoking ban, Len the caretaker had become more popular. The prof had sorted out the question of access, so Rick was not worried when Crispy Dave came bustling in and said "Young Ridd, you're not supposed to be here."

"Oh yes I am" Rick replied automatically.

"Rotten to see you" said Dave, and they both smiled.

Rick cast his eyes around the dingy room, looking for a suitable hiding place for his microphone. Only now did it occur to him that this was a serious piece of kit for the professor to be handing out like a bag of sweets. Rick took his job seriously, and he tried to keep up to date with the electronics catalogues, but this stuff looked more James Bond than High Street.

The staff room was too big for one microphone to pick up anything usable, and Rick assumed that there would be times of the day when it was full of the cacophony of strong, projecting voices vying for attention. So the central light fitting and the polystyrene ceiling tiles were out of the question. What he was looking for was a place where staff would engage in embarrassing conversations when there was little background noise. Crispy Dave coughed politely and gestured towards the two long tables he had set up at one end of the room. He gave Rick a sample report card and an instruction sheet. On the tables were neat piles of cards for each first-year tutor group. Rick remembered getting his mini report card at the end of October and naively thinking it was amazing that all his teachers knew him well enough to judge him after just two months. The guidelines for teachers Crispy Dave said was a quick check to flag up any early problems, with an attainment grade (A - E) and a score for effort (1 - 5). Rick thought this was like using a steamroller to crack a nut, but it got worse: each teacher had to write a one-line comment, and the form teacher had half a page to fill. That meant the cards could not be taken out of the room for the next three days, leaving the form teachers just Friday and the weekend to do their "bit".

Once the coast was clear, Rick taped the microphone to the underside of one of the desks, found a suspiciously handy plug socket and got out of the staff room as quickly as he could. Somehow, it all felt too easy. Just for a moment, Rick wondered whether it wasn't the gullible yokel film crew who was being played, but he decided he really didn't give a toss. He completed the set up for the mike and went to fetch his camera. He made his way to Room 14, where the the Book of Gerry Mee, Chapter 9 Verse B, foretold yet another second year German class for Mr Rossall, starting in five minutes.

The gods of misrule must have smiled on the new teachers during Chaos Day. Phil Rossall had most of his lessons in Room 14 and Ginny Reeves was immediately opposite in 13. This was prime real estate, the Hartles equivalent of Mayfair on the Monopoly board. Rick wondered where the Go Straight to Jail space was and decided it was either Statham's art room or wherever Farmer George was teaching Geography.

Whatever the standard of some of his colleagues was, Phil Rossall's classroom was a haven of peace. The bell went and his third-year class gently chanted "Auf Wiedersehen, Herr Rossall". Rick recognised several members of Statham's penis-modelling class he and Mick had filmed earlier. They acted like totally different people. Even Bird seemed to be eating out of her German teacher's hand.

As the third years filed out and the second formers waited patiently in the corridor, Rick began to wonder if he was filming in the right place. But it was too late to pull out now. The German teacher invited him into the room, shook his hand and said "Welcome to our little bit of Germany. You must be Rick."

"I suppose I must be" he replied, thoroughly nonplussed. No teacher had ever spoken to him like that.

'Please feel free to film whatever you want." he said. The next twenty minutes were spent calling the register. That was over half the lesson gone before Herr Rossall could teach them anything new.

Today was open mike day, so Rick got to film the rare full fat version of the register game. The teacher held up a large carrot and a Kinder egg. The carrot was today's comedy microphone, and the rules said that. without it, you were struck dumb. Herr Rossall handed the fantasy mike to a random pupil and addressed the class with a couple of mimed, silent sentences, which had the class giggling into their hands.

"These are twelve-year-olds" thought Rick. "By the time I was twelve, I was . . . well, never mind that now."

Rick focused on a girl in the middle row, who was blowing on the carrot and counting "eins, zwei, drei, vier". After more stifled giggles from the class, she told everyone six things about herself in German. The teacher made a great show of putting a tick for her on the register. Even to an outsider like Rick, it was obvious that she had covered her name, her age and a bit about her family and where she lived. Then she passed the mike on to someone else.

To Rick, the seemingly endless repetition was brain-numbingly boring, which was pretty ironic, given his day job. However, the class clearly found it fascinating, and they were all desperate to have a go. Rick was just about to stop recording, when he heard a familiar voice.

"Guten Tag! Ich heiße Onkel Peter . . ."

Rick had not seen that coming, although he now thought he had found an explanation for the unnaturally good behaviour of the children. The teacher and his class were obviously used to Uncle Pete "popping in for a mo". To be fair, Pete did a lot of popping, nipping and dropping in. No doubt, he had put a lot of effort into the Doktor Doktor Liesl damage limitation project. Pete very rarely got angry, but he was incandescent with fury when he thought of all the time stolen from young people, when they could have been running free, simply enjoying being kids. Education was normally quite low on Pete's list of priorities, but there was a new town twinning with Germany on the horizon, possibly with the Holy Grail: a proper language exchange, with children spending a couple of weeks as members of their host families.

As Mayor of Oxbridge, Pete was desperate to drag the sleepy town out of its isolation, and town twinning was one of his most effective weapons. The French connection had been a rip-roaring success, and the link to the Spanish twin was as old as the Pyrenees. Life in Oxbridge without the annual Sheep Run was unthinkable.

But the Town Council's attempts at finding a German partner had all ended in miserable failure. A recent visit from the mayor of a town in rural Lower Bavaria had lasted one day, when he realised just how slow the journey was from London. As the Bürgermeister said in his perfect English "If I wanted to smell cowshit all day, I could have stayed at home".

So when the twinning request came in from somewhere called Mariushütte near Dortmund, Pete grabbed it with both hands. Their letter had been in English, and he had answered in English. But it was when he tried to add a cheery little greeting in German that it struck him that he had spent innumerable hours in Liesl's lessons without picking up a single word of the language. Now he had a ridiculously energetic teacher, who knew his stuff and was happy to teach him along with the kids.

As soon as he had said his party piece, Uncle Pete handed on the carrot-mike and left as silently as he had come. Rick was impressed that the lesson didn't miss a beat. The register was completed and Mr Rossall swapped the little German flag on his desk for a Union Jack. This signified that English could now be spoken. Rick assumed the floodgates would now open to all sorts of illicit chatter. But instead it went so quiet that you could hear the sound of young people's digestive systems failing to break down some nasty little shards of Wiener Schnitzel.

The children knew roughly what was coming, but they still weren't sure if their friends were pulling their legs. The teacher rolled down the blackboard, on which was written just two words: FIRST COUSINS. Herr Rossall told them about the huge number of languages spoken around the world. He explained that, just like people, they belonged to families, and German was a close relative to English, like a first cousin.

He then rolled the blackboard again to reveal what looked like a random list of English words and phrases. Mr Rossall did not explain the rules of this new game. He simply asked if anyone would like to pick an English phrase, and a forest of hands flew up. Rick had to stop himself putting his hand up too.

"Tanya" said the teacher, pointing to a grubby street urchin on the back row. "My father" she suggested in a Woodbine croak. He said the words in German and conducted the class as they repeated what they had heard: "Mine Farter".

Next, he chose Supergeek Simon, largely for humanitarian reasons as Simon looked fit to burst.

"Please sir, Señor Mr Herr Rossall. Can I have Notebook?"

The same principle applied, with the teacher saying the German word and the class repeating what they heard: "No-tits-buch".

"Well done with the short gargling sound at the end" gloated Rossall.

The bell for the end was fast approaching, and the game of verbal ping pong speeded up.

"Fat" asked one chosen child. The teacher gave the answer, and the class chanted "dick".

"Fox" - "fux"

"Motorway exit" - "ours fart"

"Team" - "man shaft"

"Doughnut" - "crap fun"

There were plenty more words left, but someone shouted out a question without being invited, and the board was wiped before you could say Ludwig van Beethoven. The lesson ended with a bog-standard calm-down activity and the presentation of the Kinder egg to the most improved pupil.

Manipulative swine, thought Rick, pardon my Kraut. Just wait until we start to edit you.

Chapter 13 – Mop bucket

Rick couldn't get out of Phil Rossall's room quickly enough. He found it hard to order his thoughts, but he was repulsed by the near hypnotic power this upstart had over the kids of Hartles. True, Uncle Pete had a far greater hold over them, but he had earned that by years of hard work and blackmail with menaces, if that was even a thing. Rick's knowledge of the law only stretched to weed and petty larceny.

He needed some fresh air, no matter how wet it was. But after only a couple of steps in the direction of the main entrance, he heard that familiar voice singing "Mr Ridd, could you spare us a minute?"

What did your last slave die of? thought Rick. God, I really miss my brother. Still, you don't ignore Uncle Pete's voice, even if you have no clue where it's coming from. He hadn't even got as far as the staff room when he heard the voice again. "In here, sharpish" said Pete, holding open the windowless door to the cleaners' cupboard. Rick had had just about enough of this gown and dagger stuff, but he did as he was told. It was quite a squeeze, though. Neither Uncle Pete nor Professor Duckworth was exactly a lightweight, and Rick only just managed to shut the door.

The Stealth Inspector

"Now young man, we have need of your expert assistance" said Danny Duckworth in fluent Pompous.

"Sorry, Prof" Rick fired back. "We only do hetero, and you two haven't come out of the closet."

This earned him a scowl from Danny Duckworth and a rather cramped high five from Pete.

"Moving on" said Danny stiffly "let's try setting up the audio receiver and recorder I gave you. Where did you put the microphone/transmitter device?"

"You know perfectly well where I put the mike" snapped Rick. "Do you mean the little dangly thing on the wire is the transmitter?"

Danny nodded. "And it's voice activated, so you won't have to wade through hours of silence".

Despite himself, Rick let out a low whistle and asked "So where did you get this gear?"

They both spoke at once. Danny opened with "I'm sorry, but I cannot reveal . . . " and Pete blurted out "Sicknote".

Rick frowned. "So the school nurse supplied you with Military Intelligence-grade surveillance equipment?"

Pete nodded and Danny said brusquely "You should be well within range here. Uncle Peter and I will go to the target area and conduct a conversation."

The Stealth Inspector

"If you're sure you are up to it" said Rick.

Two minutes later, the would-be film maker was purring with joy. It was only audio, but it could blow the head off this place. As he walked around the building, taking still shots and random video clips to accompany the hopefully candid staff room conversations, Rick wondered again why this school was bending over backwards to help him make their suicide video. And he was still worried that he didn't feel bad about being one of the gang putting the boot in.

That's because you're an evil sod, thought Mick. Rick laughed from the sheer relief of reconnecting with his twin brother. I could murder a pie and a pint or ten, they thought in tandem.

The next day, they were both nursing headaches, so they decided to go to Plan B. They would still be well over the limit, not that there was any risk of being stopped and breathalysed. Nobody ever was. But they were forced to take a minicab home not so early that morning. The last bus had left at 7pm and the train in 1963. They couldn't crash at a friend's house, so they took the risk of crashing with Slalom Taxis. That wasn't their official name, but it was pretty accurate. A combined lack of driving ability, sobriety and functioning headlights made every journey a white-knuckle ride. The twins were particularly lucky that night, because they got Stevie Wonder to drive them. He didn't look anything like the singer, but when he started driving, the ducking

106

and rolling head movements were uncannily similar. His swaying body motion guided the car from hedge to hedge. If there had been any traffic on the roads and the taxi had a third or fourth gear, Rick thought the whole thing could be just a tad dangerous.

After some much needed sleep aboard Rocky's Rocket, the twins collected their gear from the office safe and headed straight for Hut F, the kingdom of Mop Bucket. Nominally, it was registration time, but such niceties meant nothing in the home of the Effers Club. Six out of the eight members of the mixed age Remedial Stream and their teacher Rob Burley were together. These were the only people allowed across the threshold. Occasionally, guests were invited, most notably Uncle Pete and now Rick Ridd. Where the cameras fitted into the scheme of things was unclear. Membership of the Effers Club was for life, so they got the odd walk-in like Mick. They would usually want feeding, but the class made them sing for their supper. Visitors would have to teach the class a skill they had recently picked up at work. This was what Mick had been so worried about yesterday, and with good reason. His communication difficulties were so severe that, even after all the help he had been given in Hut F, he was still at best a two sentence a day man. He had just got very good at hiding it. But two decades of verbal constipation had taken their toll, and this was the only place he could have completed such a task. Not surprisingly, the class had lapped it up. Hands on camera tuition, interspersed with salacious gossip, was always going to be a winner.

Rick still couldn't work out how he fitted in, but he didn't really care. The main thing was that it would make great television. Just look at the cast, thought Rick.

There was the teacher who was harder to read than a Shakespeare play, and whose name, as sure as death and taxis, was not Rob Burley. The class today consisted of six people aged twelve to seventeen. Another club member was in hospital for yet more anti-cancer treatment, but the prognosis was good. The class called her Baldilocks, and they couldn't wait for her to get back and continue her education with them. The eighth Effer would, according to Rob, be along soon, or possibly not. Very much present was the huge frame of an adolescent who had a rare genetic disorder, which gave him facial features the doctors, in their unfeeling way, called mongoloid. His name was Jeremy, but now he only answered to Mong the Merciless. Another older boy appeared to be asleep. Rick recognised him as Sleepy Sam. He was a Townie, from the Peters Estate. The estate was part of the London Clearance Initiative back in the '60s, when "troubled" families from problem estates were resettled as far away from the capital as possible. The thirty families who agreed to the move from North Peckham to Oxbridge seemed happy with the change, and the locals hardly even noticed them. However, there were vestiges of the bad old days, most visibly in what the experts call "dodgy parenting". Sam's inverse narcolepsy - deep sleep punctuated by rare moments of manic lucidity - was only spotted when he started primary school. His parents had described him as a quiet boy, no trouble.

The Peters estate had also been home to Bounce, a smiley girl whose mother had repeatedly dropped her on her head as a baby. The class was completed by three boys, who had achieved very little in mainstream education, and concluded that school was not for them.

This odd mixture of a class could probably not even have existed elsewhere in the country. Mong and Bounce qualified for special education, but the nearest suitable Special Schools were too far away to allow them to attend as day pupils. So they were here for social reasons, while the rest of the class had to follow the mainstream curriculum.

Except they didn't do anything of the sort. Rick and Mick got some good footage of Mop Bucket's opening talk on understanding other people. It was hard to say whether any of this was getting through to the rest of the Effers. Most were lounging around, mug of tea in hand. The teacher strung together anecdotes of how people got what they wanted by being nice to others and seeing things from their point of view.

"I just use my fists" bragged Jim, a sixteen-year-old bundle of anger.

"Right" said Rob Burley in hushed tones. "And how's that going?"

"Up before the magistrate tomorrow" laughed Al the Non-achiever. "The new one, the Missus Mayor. She'll be nice and understanding".

Amid the general laughter, the teacher drove his point home. He shook his head in mock sadness and said "That's the trouble with using your fists. You'll always come across someone with bigger fists."

He got them to put together a big round table in the exact centre of the hut. A large piece of paper appeared out of nowhere, a perfect fit for the table top.

"Can I pull the chain, please Señor?" squeaked Bounce. By this time, everyone in the class had their hands up, or rather, everyone who was awake. The teacher said "Jeremy, you pull the chain." There was some muted laughter around the room as Mong played his part in a well-rehearsed scene. "Who's Jeremy?"

"You're Jeremy" replied his teacher.

"I" the boy announced grandly "am Mong the Merciless. See me and weep". Still beaming beatifically, he reached up and pulled a cord hanging from the ceiling. Nothing seemed to happen until they had closed the blackout curtains. The tiny hole in the roof was shedding a beam of light, which focused perfectly on the big circle of paper.

"You have your cameras, we have our camera obscura" said Rob Burley proudly. Around him, there was frenetic activity, as everyone fetched chairs, pencils and crayons. It was evidently a race against the clock. This will make great television, thought Rick, they all look so keen. When everyone was ready, Rob shouted "HBs ready? Five minutes. Go!" The panorama of school, park, town and fields fascinated Rick, who was the only one seeing it for the first time. He could have watched the moving people and vehicles for hours, but the Effers had different ideas. They traced in pencil the outline of everything that moved, so that they were frozen in time. The teacher stopped them to check the figures were roughly in the right place. The real people had moved on, but that didn't matter. They could now trace everything else at their leisure.

Rob gave his class their instructions: "Trace all the other outlines, fill in the details in pencil and make up a story about one of the people in the picture, to be told to the class tomorrow."

A hand went up next to Bounce's excited face. The hand held a new pack of crayons.

"Yes, Mary Bounce" said the teacher. "Then you can colour in to your heart's content."

Jim butted in: "Colouring in, that's for spas . . . "

He didn't finish his sentence. Instead, he shot a nervous glance towards the door, which had the only uncurtained window in the hut. Rick had Jim's face in tight close-up, and it was quite clear that the boy didn't like what he saw. Oddly, Mick had his camera trained on a dark corner of the hut, where a rectangular plastic box was standing. It had two bucket-shaped holes moulded into it, one of which was playing host to a rather disreputable mop.

Then the chanting started "Mop Bucket, Mop Bucket, Mop Bucket . . . "

The whole class was shouting and stamping their feet to the same rhythm. Strangely, that included Jim, until he remembered why they were all chanting. When the teacher had managed to restore order, he asked Jim what he had done wrong.

"Been disrespectful to other members of the club, haven't I?" said Jim miserably. Rick thought he had given this spiel many times before. "But sir" Jim pleaded "it's raining outside.

"Where else is it supposed to rain?" asked a voice from the other end of the hut. By the time people had turned round to look at him, Sam was fast asleep again.

Rob Burley smiled at Jim sympathetically and said "If you do it right, you can come in for lunch. Miss Bounce, what are we cooking today?"

"Thingie of lamb" beamed Bounce.

"Rack of lamb" said Al, forgetting to be the non-achiever. "That should go well with the Primitivo".

"Lamb with red wine?" sang a new voice by the door "That's for peasants. Let's break out the Alberiño". The eighth member of the Effers Club had come in without being noticed.

"Don't let us keep you, Jim" said Molly Stidworth, opening the door.

Rick focused on Jim as he picked up the bucket and trudged through the foul weather to the centre of the playground. There he turned the bucket upside down and stood on it, as if he were a statue and this was his plinth. He stood there stoically in the lashing rain, facing the hut, awaiting further instructions.

Chapter 14 – Bringing up Oxbridge

It may not have been a Hollywood style home theatre, but Jan Ridd had somewhere he could show his films. A draughty barn with hard wooden chairs would do just fine, if you didn't mind the smell of pigs. Phil Rossall had been intrigued by his invitation to a viewing of the first cut of Bringing Up Oxbridge, followed by Sunday lunch and "discussion". It was only a few days since the twins had finished filming and he was surprised that anything decent could have been produced so quickly. Mind you, the Ridd family was more used to producing the indecent. Someone had lent him a copy of Down Mammary Lane, and he was so bored, his mind started to wander. He remembered thinking "We used to have a coffee table like that". He doubted much editing had been going on there.

Looking around the audience, he was puzzled about why he had been invited. In addition to the host Jan Ridd, the ubiquitous Uncle Pete was sitting in the front row with Professor Danny Duckworth. Behind them sat the school nurse Sicknote. The other deputy Gerry Mee and Rob Burley, alias Mop Bucket, completed the second row, with Ginny Reeves joining him on the back row, along with two studenty types called Stuart and Zara.

The Stealth Inspector

Phil's doubts about the technical competence of the film makers were soon proved to be unfounded. The images were crystal clear, the sound was crisp, and the editing was brutally efficient. If someone had wanted to string together the most embarrassing scenes of life in Hartles School, and ruthlessly strip them of all context, they could not have done a better job. Jan Ridd had told his audience in preamble that he had just been elected Acting Chair of Governors, and now he was tearing his school into quivering shreds. Phil cringed as he watched this half hour of car crash TV.

The shockumentary opened with a few snippets from interviews. From 5 Ridd we learned of the wide scale of bullying and racketeering in the lower school. The face shots were skilfully blended with footage of playground intimidation. In case this was all too subtle, there were also a few impressionistic shots of the sextuplets beating up a first year boy, whose school uniform appeared to be covered in tomato ketchup.

Another mini-interview with Bates the PE teacher told the story of the attempted lynching as if it had happened yesterday. While Bates droned on about his heroic part in saving a boy from certain death at the hands of a gang of Hartles savages, the audience was treated to out of focus shots of uniformed thugs running towards a large oak tree. Just to make sure that the hard of thinking were still following his narrative, Jan had edited in the occasional super-closeup of rope and a red tinted neck.

Then came the scene Phil Rossall had been secretly dreading. There he was, the grinning German teacher, conducting a class of twelve-year-olds as they shouted lustily "Fart, Dick, No Tits, Man Shaft". As he sat and cringed at the back of the makeshift cinema, Phil realised just how bad this would look to the outside viewer. There was no context. The vicious editing implied that it was somehow connected to the attempted lynching in the previous scene. And then Phil realised that the demonic editor was going to use his little soundbite over and over again, like a Wagnerian leitmotif. He was soon proved right, but his tormentor Jan had finessed it by using slightly different clips each time, giving the impression that this was all that ever happened in Phil's German lessons.

Even the cock-and-balls-up of the third year Art lesson didn't escape the Jan Ridd treatment. Not content with the nudity and lewdity of the original version, Jan had given the impression that Statham was in control like a proper teacher, and that sketching male genitalia was part of the curriculum at Hartles School. The corridor display cases full of pottery willies had been a particularly nice touch.

Phil knew about some of the other likely scenes, but that didn't make them any less shocking when given the Jan Ridd treatment. He had been expecting to see a boy standing on an upturned

116

bucket in the pouring rain, but he had not been prepared for the row of grinning people - teacher and pupils - standing by the windows and raising their wine glasses in a cheery toast to their miserable, sodden victim.

A string of banal extracts from a variety of classes led to what Phil thought was an exemplary first year history lesson. The teacher allowed a small boy near the back to ask a question. Incongruously, a much larger, older girl was sitting behind him, doing her knitting. The boy squeaked something inaudible, whereupon the girl launched a round-arm swing at his right ear. The class didn't see anything, but Jan's edit showed the teacher giving the girl a smile and a wink. Even more incongruously, to Phil's mind, was that this was unmistakably the same girl who had been drinking wine while that poor boy was being given the water bucket treatment.

Phil was still at a loss about what the documentary was supposed to achieve, and the next segment didn't help him one bit. Pictures of the main entrance and the school office alternated with slow panning shots of corridors and the empty staff room. The camera lingered lovingly over the tables at one end of the room, showing in artfully hazy closeup the piles of first year report cards that covered them.

But the visuals were not the point. The audience was now treated to the joys of eavesdropping.

Voices were to be heard from the staff room. Jan had helpfully added subtitles, but he had drawn the line at naming the speakers, which for some reason made the whole thing even worse. Phil recognised Ginny Reeves playing the part of the naive probationer, asking her colleagues the same questions over and over again:

"What do I do with these report cards?"

"How can I score children I don't know yet?"

"What sort of things can I write in the Comment box?"

Ginny played the role of damsel in distress to perfection, and Phil couldn't help feeling a bit jealous. Ginny was going to come out of this shambles a lot better than he was.

Phil had always thought the word "toe-curling" was an empty cliché, but some of the answers to Ginny's queries were making his toes ball up and hide in what he thought must be the feetal position.

One disembodied voice managed to convey a perfect blend of condescension and lechery:

"You are quite right, my dear, we have only been teaching them a couple of months. I don't know their names yet, so I give them the middle mark C3 Satis. That's C for attainment, 3 for effort and, if you write big enough, you don't even have to use the whole word "Satisfactory". If I do know them or an older sibling, I sometimes throw in the odd

"Working well" or "could do better". I find this system works with other year groups too. You can't be expected to know all the little blighters".

A vaguely Scottish voice was heard telling Ginny about the zigzag method of scoring. "I start with A1 for the first name on the list, then go down B2, C3, D4 and E5. And then it's back up the roller coaster to A1. If I'm in a good mood, I miss out E5. Kids tend to get grounded for that. But generally I leave it in, to show I'm not a soft touch."

The next voice belonged to a female Games teacher. She told Ginny about the problem she had with writing reports. "We teach everyone in the school. I only know the kids in the school teams. They get B2. For the rest, it's C2. I don't like it, but at least it's better than the Knuckle Draggers".

"Who are the Knuckle Draggers?" asked Ginny, as if she didn't already know.

"Three of my esteemed PE colleagues" said her informant. "They get easily bored writing reports. They're not comfortable with anything in their hands that's smaller than a javelin. So they make it into a game. This time round, it's Mugshots. This involves three coffee mugs, two sets of class reports and a couple of bottles of tequila. Whoever finishes a class first shouts "Tequila" in a silly Mexican accent and drains his mug. His playmates follow suit, and so on literally ad nauseam."

Phil wondered whether this was why they called this horror film Bringing Up Oxbridge. But he had lost the ability to think for himself. Like a rubbernecker passing the scene of a motorway crash, he had no choice but to turn his head and gawp. Ginny's disembodied voice was already lining up it's next victim, a seasoned warrior who had survived many a year in the chalk trenches.

"I think I'm all right with these cards" she said hesitantly, as if she knew that she was pushing her luck "but how will I cope with the long comments needed for full reports later in the year?"

The old soldier answered "I'm sure you will know them much better by then. You English teachers usually do."

"But I might not know what to write" said Ginny in mock anguish. She was definitely fishing now, but the old lag didn't seem to notice.

"Well we have a couple of handy tools, if you ever get stuck for something to say. Some colleagues use them all the time". His voice went down to a conspiratorial whisper. Unfortunately, Phil was still able to follow with the subtitles. He heard two heavy objects landing on the table.

"These" he confided "are the gift of our former Religious Studies teacher. He left the school years ago, but he also left us this notebook. First there's a collection of stupid things teachers say, like Bates asking someone how you spell PE. But this section .

.. er . . . here gives the would-be report writer some useful phrases to help them on their way. There's lots of alternatives to the old clichéd ways of saying "Well done". But it's the negative comments that have proved the most popular. Take a look at some of these."

"Sorry" said Ginny "I must have left my glasses on my desk. Can you read me a few?"

The veteran walked straight into the trap. "How about:

This child is a perambulating waste of space.

Young X has delusions of adequacy.

She would be out of her depth in a car park puddle.

There's pages of them. You get the general idea?"

"And what's this clunky little thing?" asked Ginny. "It looks like a mini slot machine."

Her victim laughed. "That's exactly what it is. It's a Random Jargon Generator. It has three spools of education-speak, and all you do is pull this little lever like so. You get your three random words, add the odd verb or conjunction, and Fanny is very much your aunt."

Phil breathed a sigh of relief when the film went back to its catalogue of awful lessons. But the Geography lesson was a new lowlight. At least, Phil assumed it was Geography. Farmer George waxing lyrical on the uses of the Wellington boot would have been embarrassing at the best of times. In the hands of a master editor like Jan Ridd, it sounded positively obscene.

Just when Phil thought things couldn't get any worse, they did. Sitting next to him in the makeshift cinema, Ginny had her head in her hands. She couldn't watch as the camera followed her into the Headteacher's office, where two women were sitting at one end of a very shiny table.

"Do sit down" said Liz Fairfax, the Head's PA. That's one mystery solved, thought Phil. He had been trying to work out where he had heard Liz's cut-glass accent before. Now he remembered. She had conducted his job interview over the phone. He thought at the time that the interview was rather strange, but he never suspected that he been given this job by the secretary.

The Headmistress smiled benignly as Liz Fairfax pointed to a large painting on the wall.

"I see you're admiring the portrait of Don Ron" said the PA. The Head whispered something in her ear and they both giggled like schoolgirls. Liz continued "The Lady says they have the Hartles family look: no chin, sunken teeth, whispy hair".

"Sorry if this sounds rude" said Ginny "but do you always speak for the Headmistress?"

"I speak for her, deal with the paperwork and do the odd phonetic transcript for speeches."

"So you help her with her English?" persisted Ginny.

"Good Lord, no" Liz laughed "the Mistress doesn't speak any English."

The demonic editor made sure he gave the Headteacher the final word. Sitting there with both thumbs up, she grinned toothlessly down the lens of the camera and said "Hartles eschool bery good".

Chapter 15 - Don't panic! Don't panic!

Phil Rossall just sat there in the dark, sharing in the stunned silence. When the lights came on, the silence was replaced by a communal groan. Of course, Jan Ridd's reaction was somewhat different. As he stood up to address the audience, his face was beaming with pride. The subtext was clear for all to read: you wanted a hatchet job, and that's what you got. The assembled guests didn't look as if they had asked for it, with the exception of Professor Danny Duckworth, who seemed to Phil to be feeding off the other people's misery, like a seedy little vampire.

Fortunately, Jan knew the way to cheer them up. "Lunch will be served in the big kitchen. Just follow your nose and you'll find it. My wife Mother Earth and her kid sister have roasted a young pig and made a plum pudding. The vegetarian option is Ritz crackers and an apple."

This is more like it, thought Phil. Mother Earth had a reputation for her cooking, to which her husband's barrel-shaped body clearly bore witness. She invited her guests to come up to the huge inglenook fireplace and cut themselves a few pieces off the spit-roasted animal. Her "kid sister" danced in and out, fetching veg and bottles of dry white

Alsace Gewürztraminer. She and Mother Earth linked arms and responded to the enthusiastic applause with a combined bow and curtsy. There may have been a twenty-year age gap between the sisters, but they were like two peas in a pod.

"I have chosen something fruity but dry to go with this pig on its final journey." said Molly Stidworth. "White wine, because pork with red wine is for peasants."

Several diners joined in the refrain. Bloody hell, thought Phil, she's only fifteen, and she's already got her own catchphrase.

"Enjoy your lunch, 'cos you've got the professor next. In the meantime," she raised her glass for a toast "May the halls be alive with the sound of crackling!"

After everything had been cleared away, they stayed where they were for the meeting. As threatened, Professor Danny Duckworth took the lead. Phil thought he was looking a little greyer and madder by the day.

"I hope you enjoyed our little film" he started, only to be greeted with stony silence. "I think it will do its job very nicely."

"But when it comes out, we'll be a laughing stock" shouted Mop Bucket.

"Oh, I wouldn't worry about it going public" replied Danny calmly. "With any luck, it will never see the light of day."

Now there was a serious rumble of discontent from around the table. The postprandial spirit of goodwill had not lasted long. Ginny Reeves was first out of the blocks.

"Do you mean we went through all that for nothing?" she shouted at Danny. "That film made me look like the Wicked Witch of the South West!"

In Phil's opinion, Danny replied a little too quickly and perhaps a tad rashly "Then it's just as well it may never see the light of day."

This was evidently the wrong thing to say. Around the table, voices were raised, leftover cutlery brandished. Only Uncle Pete seemed unaffected by the general hubbub, smiling serenely and sipping the last of Molly's wine. Suddenly, Jan Ridd whistled as only a hill-farming shepherd can whistle. The silence that followed was punctuated by tinkling glass and the baying of dogs in the yard.

"I think we got off on the wrong foot" said Jan in a conciliatory tone. "Let's come back to the topic of the film later. Please listen to the professor. He has something important to say."

There was still some discontented murbling, but Danny started anyway.

"Friends, I have some good news and some bad news. A letter is on its way to the Head, informing her that the school will have an Ofsted inspection in the second week of February, immediately before the half term break."

There was some gentle laughter around the table. This seemed to unnerve the professor, who was clearly unaware that he had said anything funny. When Uncle Pete had controlled his fit of girlish giggles, Danny continued, "But we will be ready. And I can guarantee you that we will achieve the highest grade. Hartles School will be judged to be Outstanding!"

"And what was the good news?" asked Phil.

More laughter, this time a little less restrained. Danny looked mortified. Why were they laughing at his life's work?

Then it was Molly's turn. What was this teenager even doing here, Phil asked himself. Not in Jan's house. Unlikely as it seemed, she was the sixty-year-old's sister in law. But what was she doing in this meeting? Phil resolved to find out more about her.

"We have been outstanding for years" Molly teased. "Mop Bucket always has someone out standing in the rain."

"That's not fair, Molls" answered the smiling Rob Burley. "It's not always raining."

Uncle Pete was the next to try his luck.

"What my friend the professor is trying to say is that our Hartles can get the status of an excellent school and provide a huge boost to the local economy. He's the expert, so we should shut up and do what he says."

Danny was finally able to go through his master plan. But first, he gave them a potted history of Ofsted. Danny was warming to his task. After all, this was his life's work. Phil thought he could see the fanaticism in Danny's eyes, with maybe just a hint of paranoia.

"So what Ofsted is looking for" he continued "are the three Cs: Compliance, Consistency and Coherence. Compliance is about following government guidance as if it was the Ten Commandments, having school policies in line with every aspect of the guidelines and being able to prove to the inspectors that everything you do lies within that framework."

"Lies being the operative word" chipped in Mop Bucket.

Far from being annoyed, Danny seemed delighted with the intervention. "Give that man a cigar!" he shouted. It's impossible for a school focused on providing a good education for its children to keep up with the stream of edicts coming down from local and national government. For instance, what is Hartles School's policy on modern slavery, and how is that policy implemented? Do you conduct regular risk assessments for homelessness? Do you have an influenza plan? The answer is obviously no, but Ofsted sets great store by this stuff, because it is easy to assess. Fortunately, you don't have to worry, because I will sort it all out for you. Compliance is my middle name."

"That's handy" muttered Ginny.

"Handy for you" said Danny smugly. He pressed on "The second C is Consistency. Ofsted favours the Macdonalds system of quality assurance. The product may be anaemic mince trapped in an insipid sweet bun, it may be tasteless pap, but it is guaranteed to be the same tasteless pap, whether you are in Washington or Ouagadougou. You won't get dogburgers or dysentery, but you will miss out on delicious real food. For all its rhetoric on recognising excellence, the way Ofsted scores quality of teaching favours consistent mediocrity over individual brilliance. And the score card never lies. But, my friends, it can be *lied to*. That is where I can help you."

"But why do you want to help us?" asked Ginny, now in full rebel mode, "and what's in it for you?"

"My aim is to improve Ofsted inspections." Danny answered calmly. "If I can help my good friend Uncle Pete and his colleagues along the way, so much the better. Now, as I was saying, Ofsted are looking for three Cs, and the last of these is Coherence. This is all marketing speak about the organisation making a holistic offer to stakeholders, which always reminds me of vampire hunters. Even more confusingly, the inspection handbook" Danny held up a black leather folder "talks about pupils and parents being on board, but on board what? I think the best word for this section is Ethos, but that doesn't begin with a C. There are loads of points going for this, and some of the best schools in the country miss out on them. I can help you manufacture a new ethos and make it look like you have had it for ages. So yes, we can cheat and lie to make Hartles School outstanding."

"But what in the Devil's sock drawer has any of this to do with the film?" shouted Ginny. "You remember, the cringefest that came between Hello and Lunch?"

Danny responded with a smug smile "The film is an integral part of the plan, but I don't want to divulge at this stage how we will use it. For the time being, I am asking you to trust me."

Ginny looked as if she was just about to explode, so Phil thought it wise to move things on a bit.

"I'm still a newcomer here" he said, "and I am already in love with Hartles School. But even I know it's not Outstanding by any objective measure. My question is: why do we need to get the top mark from Mr Ofsted? It's not like we're in some London suburb, where parents have a genuine choice between schools. We're the only secondary school within reach, and there's not even a private option since they closed down Dotheboys Hall, I mean Frickley Park. And there's never been anything for the girls. So why all this effort to make us look Outstanding?"

Uncle Pete got to his feet, clearly annoyed. "There are lots of reasons why it would be good for the school" he said hotly. "More money for staffing and equipment. And Don Ron wants it. But, as Mayor, I am more excited about the opportunities for the town and area. Sicknote, would you care to say a few words?"

"No"

"Anyway" announced Jan Ridd, fixing Phil and Ginny with a steely stare, "we have discussed this enough for the time being. Let's have a tot of Mother Earth's famous apple brandy and set the world to rights."

The meeting broke up, but Phil was still worried about Ginny. She was glaring at Danny, with steam practically coming out of her ears. Phil thought it wise to keep her away from the professor until she had calmed down. She meekly allowed herself to be led towards the fireplace, where Mother Earth was standing, chatting to her kid sister.

After they had thanked their hostess, Phil asked if he could borrow her sister for a while. Ginny looked confused, but at least the distraction manoeuvre seemed to be working. Molly didn't seem at all confused.

"I was wondering how long it would take you" confided Molly with a most undeferential smile. "Let's go into the snug. It'll be quieter in there. You'd better bring Miss Reeves with you. She looks like she's about to commit GBH, and this is an ABH-only household."

The two teachers meekly followed the fifteen-year-old to a small room with three leather armchairs set around a coffee table. Waiting for them were cups of steaming coffee, balloon-shaped brandy glasses and a bottle barely discernible through decades of dust. Phil hated to be so predictable, and it must have shown in his face.

"Don't worry" Molly said, gleefully adding insult to injury, "This sort of clairvoyance stunt is still way beyond me. It's just my mentor Sicknote showing off. She said you would have some questions, and she asked me to answer them in private, only for the ears of the Duckworth recruits, as she put it. So what do you want to know?"

Phil was still irritated about being taken for granted. Was he really so easy to read? He knew he was no match for Sicknote, but maybe he could wipe the grin off this smug teenager's face.

Phil went straight in for the kill: "Why didn't you choose an Alsace Riesling for the hog roast?"

Ginny was looking at him as if he had fallen from the sky. She whispered vehemently in Phil's ear "Of all the questions you could have asked, why .... " She cast a glance at Molly and saw the girl's face go through a series of contortions, as if she were trying on masks in a party shop. She made several attempts at starting a reply, then she gave up and waited for the next question.

Phil felt bad about being cruel, but that didn't stop him putting the boot in. "Tell me about Small Town Churn" he said.

"Sicknote warned me about you" 'Molly replied. "But not here. Why don't the two of you come to Rockpool House tomorrow at six, and I'll try to answer both of your questions."

Phil nodded, but Ginny looked more confused than ever. Molly took a swig of her brandy. "Come on, Phil" she teased. "I bet you can't make it three hits in a row".

Phil tried the obvious tack. "How do you get away with it all?" he enquired. Ginny clearly wanted to know that too. "You swan in and out of lessons at will. You're Fourth Year age, but your name's not on any of the registers. You beat up your brother and drink wine with Mong the Merciless, seemingly in collusion with your teachers. You call me . . ."

Phil stopped speaking and watched Molly dissolve into fits of helpless laughter.

"You thought . . ." she managed to blurt out eventually. "You thought I was a pupil at Hartles School, didn't you?"

"Well, yes" stuttered Ginny and Phil simultaneously.

"Definitely a point back for me." said Molly. "I'll tell you the tale tomorrow."

Chapter 16 – The wonders of churning

Ginny and Phil arrived chez Sicknote on the stroke of six. It was Molly who answered the door.

"Hi guys," she cooed mock-innocently "Sickie's got you well trained, I see. She's away in her other house playing happy families with her girlfriend."

"She's got another house?" enquired Ginny. That was not the question that immediately sprang to Phil's mind.

Molly led them through an immaculate Georgian drawing room and a stately period dining room to a large kitchen. "Welcome to the servants' quarters of Rockpool House" she said. "This is where the plebs hang out, which is fine by me. I wouldn't want to spill anything on one of her fine carpets. That would be bad for my life expectancy.

"Sick said it was to be full disclosure about Small Town Churn and about my own minor role in the enterprise. I also owe you both an answer to the question I dodged yesterday concerning my bonkers relationship with Hartles School. Ginny, your query about Sicknote's houses is as good a place to start as any. But first I suspect I am going to eat humble pie."

Molly walked over to the venerable Aga and took out a steaming hunk of yesterday's pork. Then she fetched two tall bottles from a wine cooler. The teenager expertly uncorked the unlabelled bottles and poured a generous measure into three red-stemmed glasses. She did the same with the other bottle and green glasses.

After a few mouthfuls of the delicious pork, Molly said "Okay, Ginny, you're in charge. What should we do next?"

Ginny took a good swig from her red glass, and the other two followed suit. "Lovely and flowery". Ginny sounded hesitant, as if she was being tested. "Is this the wine we had yesterday?"

The others nodded, like donkeys in an oilfield. "So this green glass must be the new one, the . . . Riesling" ventured Ginny. There was more nodding, followed by munching and crackling. When the three of them were able to speak again, Ginny raised her green glass in a silent toast and they all drank.

"Wow" said Ginny.

"Oh" said Molly, turning beetroot red.

"Ow" cried Phil, looking accusingly at Ginny. "Got quite a kick, this wine."

"Thanks for the solidarity, Ginny" said Molly meekly "but I had it coming. I was getting sloppy and arrogant. Anyway, I owe you some explanations."

Molly's mood brightened suddenly. "Sicknote owns this house, which has a ballroom and twelve bedrooms. She also owns the Erdington estate, with its Palladian stately home, Capability Brown deer park and nine cottages set in woodland, so private and off grid that next to nobody even knows they exist."

"I thought some aristocrat lived up in Erdington" Phil chipped in.

"You mean Lady Georgette, Marchioness of Erdington and Cotter. Marshmallow, as we call her, received a double body blow on a single day. Death Duty and a builder's estimate for a new roof arrived in the morning and Sicknote came in the afternoon. Suddenly, Marshmallow was no longer a million pounds in debt. She had lost a husband and gained a wife. There was nothing in writing, but Marsh gets to act the lady of the manor for the rest of her life, and the two of them can play happy families to their hearts' content. Sicknote now owns a sort of private hamlet, but with each house totally isolated from the others. Add in a market garden, ten outbuildings and a small dairy farm, and Sickie is ready for business."

Phil was starting to see the odd chink of light. "So this fabulous bargain purchase was the asset she needed to start a business exploiting small town churn?" he ventured. "I have no idea what that is, but I am guessing it's got nothing to do with dairy farming."

"Yes" said Molly "small town or rural churn is the process in which the brightest young talent has to leave their home area to study and work elsewhere, and is replaced by talent from the outside. The theory is that people like me and my terrible brother will leave Oxbridge for good, creating a talent vacuum, which will miraculously draw in geniuses seeking isolation and a better quality of life in our beautiful part of the world.

"Nice theory, you may think, if rather boring. The problem is there's not much evidence that it works in real life. The brain drain bit is true enough, but it usually results in isolated places gradually becoming dumber. The local genius gene pool shrinks to a murky puddle, and the birth rate cannot keep up, despite the best efforts of people like my brother-in-law Jan."

Molly took another bite of pork and swig of Riesling, which seemed to depress her all over again.

When she was ready, she checked that Ginny's and Phil's eyes hadn't glazed over. Molly continued, "Of course, there's a lot more to it than that, but I can't be arsed to tell you everything. What you need to know is that Dame Sicknote found a way to make churn work."

Molly had another sip of wine, shook her head slowly and said "I noted, Phil, your use of the word assets. Ginny, you may not know that spies call their informants and agents assets."

"Gee, thanks" snarled Ginny "I just love being patronised by teenagers."

"Anyway," Molly continued, visibly shaken, "part of Sicknote's job at MI6 was to rescue compromised assets from all over the world, and settle them and their families in the UK. The procedure is similar to the police witness protection scheme, only much more arduous and dangerous.

"As you can imagine, it's not easy for a foreigner to get a new identity and back story, blend in and avoid being assassinated by dodgy-looking tourists. Sickie became a past mistress at resettling retired spooks, and she found the perfect spot to do it. Not the anonymous big city expat hotspots, but the wide-open spaces around a town nobody's heard of, where nobody bothers you.

"Sicknote's genius was in combining the ideas of resettlement and small rural town churn. She also recognised a yawning gap in the market. It was not only spies that wanted to disappear and start their lives over again. Her clients have so far included people who have been damaged by the cult of celebrity, hounded by the intrusive media. Musicians, authors, chess grand masters, the list is endless. They crave anonymity, and they are willing to pay Sicknote a shitload of money for the privilege. Some just need a few months' respite, some may well be lifers. Do you remember Cal Climo?"

"We are studying his lyrics on his final album *Out in the Rain* in my A level English group. Such a sensitive touch" enthused Ginny. "No wonder he was touted to be the next Poet Laureate."

"I remember him" added Phil "for his long blond hair, his guitar playing and his beautiful voice. But why are we talking about him? He died years ago."

"Really?" countered Molly "And what was his biggest hit?"

"*Camera Obscura*" the two teachers replied in unison. Or, rather, they started together, but Phil's voice soon trailed off into silence.

"You're making this up" croaked Phil. "Are you seriously suggesting that a dark-haired, brown-eyed, middle-aged Special Needs teacher from this no-horse backwater of a town is actually a global superstar?"

Ginny still looked confused. "You're telling me that Mop Bucket is actually Cal Climo?" She pointed an accusing finger at Molly. "Why didn't you just come out and say so?"

Molly smiled. "I didn't want to patronise you" she said and moved swiftly on. "In many ways, it was Cal Climo who was the fiction. I mean, the prodigious talent, the modesty, the vulnerability: they were all real. But the hair was a blond wig, and the dark blue eyes came courtesy of very expensive American contact lenses. The back story about him being the son of an impoverished Cornish trawlerman was nonsense, and his home village of St Ware in Harland didn't even exist. No wonder he was so reluctant to speak of his childhood. All this was dreamt up by his agent and PR disaster Harry G. It's typical of Mops - I mean Cal - that he knew full well how incompetent Harry was, but he kept him on, because he didn't want to hurt his feelings. It didn't exactly hurt his agent's bank balance either. Harry still gets ten percent of Cal's royalties, which makes him a millionaire, twenty times over. Cal was a trusting soul, easily led. But even he drew the line at putting on a fake Cornish accent."

Molly smiled and continued "Joseph John Hanley was born in St Ives about forty years ago. No, not that St Ives. This is the one not too far from Cambridge. He was known as Johnno to his few friends. He was shy, but he was brave enough to run away to London at the age of fourteen. When he was playing his guitar and singing in that soulful voice, Johnno Hanley became someone else. Cal Climo, in fact."

"But how did he get from Cal the musical megastar to Mop Bucket, the remedial teacher?" Phil enquired.

"And, more to the point, why?" Ginny added. Phil decided to ignore her rudeness. He was glad that his colleague was enthusiastically engaging with the search for a little clarity.

"It's a long story," Molly sighed. "Not the classic rock star catalogue of drugs and booze. Cal didn't have an addictive personality. Maybe it would have been better if he had. Touring, writing and media intrusion took their toll on this gentle soul. One day, he woke up and Cal Climo was dead. Johnno Hanley had disappeared long before. The man left over suffered a nervous breakdown so severe that he spent the next few years as a silent wreck, staring out of the windows of an exclusive health clinic.

"And there he would still be but for Sicknote. She was in the clinic visiting an asset plucked from the streets of Moscow, who was drying out from decades of vodka abuse. Nobody knew the real identity of the silent man by the window, least of all the patient himself. Sickie had a hunch, but it seemed far-fetched even to a seasoned spy like her. She tells me she is a super-recogniser, which apparently is a thing, and is very useful in the Land of Spooks. Not put off by appearances, she did her research on the database that doesn't officially exist, and brought a guitar to his private room. No further proof was necessary.

"But Sicknote did not throw him back to the wolves by resurrecting Cal Climo. He was a sensitive and deeply damaged man. Instead, she filled the void

142

inside him with the fictitious history of an inspirational teacher called Rob Burley."

"You love him, don't you?" whispered Ginny.

"He has been like a father to me, far more than bloody Pyrex ever was. Anyway" Molly continued, "by the time the newborn Rob Burley was fit to travel, Sick was already thick as thieves with the three people that mattered in and around Shambles by the Sea: Uncle Pete, Don Ron and the Marchioness Marshmallow. Rob was fitted in seamlessly as a friend and colleague who was recuperating from a long illness."

"Does Rob know he used to be Cal Climo?" asked Ginny eagerly.

"No," Molly replied with a flash of anger. "And he must never find out. The shock might cause another nervous breakdown, one from which he might never recover. Sicknote has protected him as only a master spy-handler could. He is happy to be Rob Burley, and he loves being Mop Bucket."

"So why are you telling us?" Ginny persisted.

"Search me" said Molly vehemently. "Sick told me to. Why we should risk shattering such a fragile peace is beyond me. I trust you, Ginny, but . . . "

Phil interrupted her "Ok, Molly, I get the picture. You are Mop/Rob/Cal/Johnno's friend, and you want to protect him. Well, his secret is safe with me. Hold on a minute, I think I know why Sicknote wanted us to speak to you. You're more than Mop Bucket's friend, aren't you?"

Molly was on the verge of tears. "I don't know what you . . . "

"You're his Churn Buddy, aren't you?" said Phil.

"You make it sound sordid". Molly was crying softly now. "It's a beautiful thing. Mops helps me build my life and I help him rebuild his."

"It's alright" Ginny intervened, with a sideways glance at Phil. "We are only trying to understand. We haven't heard the story of your life yet."

"Well, I'm not telling him!" cried Molly, finally in full teenager mode.

"Are you sure you want me to mention that to Sicknote?" Phil whispered.

"I hate you." said Molly. You'll get my story, but not today."

"It's Ok, Molly" Phil continued in a more conciliatory tone. "I think I know what's going on. All you have to do is nod or shake your head. I think Sicknote's business model is sound. There are plenty of people who want to drop off the face of the earth, if only for a while. They are willing to pay a lot of money for a period of anonymity."

Phil paused to check on Molly, who had sat down in the lotus position on the floor. Her mood had transformed itself into a sort of smiley, nodding

144

contentment now that there was a grown-up in charge.

Phil carried on: "Things were going swimmingly. Sicknote had found her gap in the market. And then she discovered a gap in her own market. The young ones and the oldies were no problem, but where were the lucrative thirty to fifty-year-olds?"

By now, Molly was smiling and clapping silently. She looked up at Ginny and whispered "I know for a fact that Sick never told him any of this."

Phil pressed on, "So she did some more spooky-style research and found the main issue for the middle age group was their children. Sicknote knew that this segment of her market would want to take their core families with them to Offgridia. That's why she had the larger cottages ready for them. But there was one fly in the ointment: education."

"Ooh, you're good" giggled Molly. "It took me ages to figure that out. I'm impressed. Although I still hate you."

Now Phil was smiling too. "Sicknote's escape package was very tempting, but if you have school-age kids, your priorities are different. They need to share your new identity for an unspecified period, so you need them with you. Boarding school would be a security disaster. But you would want a guarantee of a halfway decent school within reach."

Phil paused for a sip of warm Riesling.

"Go on!" urged Ginny.

"You know, I think I prefer the Gewürztraminer" said Phil, swiftly moving his shins out of kicking range.

"For Sicknote's business, primary schools weren't too much of a problem, but the secondary sector was a different matter. The only private school was closed, and wouldn't reopen until paedophilia was legalised. So the only option was . . ."

"Crap?" ventured Molly.

"Hartles" continued Phil. "Of course, Sicknote's prospective clients had no idea how dysfunctional Hartles School really was. The few snippets about it in the public domain were not exactly encouraging. Like a true businesswoman, Sicknote had no interest in improving the school. But she was still missing out on a valuable income stream."

Phil paused for dramatic effect, then went in for the coup de grace:

"So what did Sicknote need to reassure the pushy parents and fill the gaping hole in her client base?"

It was a purely rhetorical question. He answered it himself.

"She needed a quick fix". The others shouted "Olé"

"She needed something authoritative, impartial and official". "Olé"

"She needed Ofsted". "Olé"

The Stealth Inspector

Phil waved his arms to conduct the chorus as they all shouted "She needed OUTSTANDING".

Chapter 17 – Human sacrifice

Professor Danny Duckworth was worried. He could not decide whether he was concerned about specific things or about the world in general. After a row of sleepless nights, he came to the conclusion that he was specifically worried about everything. Danny was no good at introspection, but even he realised that things could not go on like this. He felt like he was burning the candle at both ends, tormented by the noise of breaking crockery as he tried to keep too many plates spinning. This only served to remind him that he was also useless at metaphors. He was trying to conjure up an image of a man on the edge of a nervous breakdown, and the best he could do was Greek restaurant.

But Danny had more to fret about than insomnia, depression and his inability to concentrate on academic work. His recent experiences at the University of East Anglia had led him to believe that he was neglecting his students and his research. He was so desperate that he asked his wife for advice, breaking a habit which had lasted most of their twenty-two years of marriage. She suggested asking his employers for a sabbatical. He eventually managed to swing a four-month break for research into the assessment of teacher and school performance. The University was eager to see some published research from one of its academic stars.

That ought to have lifted Danny's mood, but he could not shake off the feeling that he was the victim of some sort of conspiracy. Admittedly, he had harboured similar feelings on and off for years, which just gave him another thing to be anxious about. Basically, he was paranoid about being paranoid. Even his wife's helpful intervention seemed vaguely sinister. He thought she was just a bit too keen to pack him off to Devonset. He didn't suspect infidelity: Honey had the sex drive of a dead mule. If it didn't involve a tennis racket or brunch, she wasn't interested. Anyway, what sort of a name was Honey Duckworth? Danny thought she sounded like the posh bird who gets killed after eighteen minutes of a Bond film. What was wrong with her real name: Janet?

But the main fodder for his paranoia came from Oxbridlesturridge, as the outside world called it. Danny thought he had the whole thing sewn up when he had befriended Uncle Pete Smythe. Pete was charming and funny but, above all, he was the main man in both Oxbridge and Hartles School. Danny still believed that nothing important could happen there without Pete's approval. And Danny was reassured by the fact that he had his friend's enthusiastic support for Operation Outstanding.

However, the more he found out about Hartles, the less he understood about where the true power lay. Uncle Pete was an important ally both as mayor and as de facto headteacher, but he was alarmingly childlike and he didn't really believe in education. There seemed to Danny's febrile mind to be someone else pulling the strings. And Danny was starting to feel like he was just one of the puppets.

This is not the time to lose the plot, he decided. Preparations for the Ofsted inspection were going swimmingly. Somehow or other, he had been given the right to choose the members of the Ofsted inspectorate who would carry out the inspection of Hartles School in February. To say that this was a major step towards the success of his project would be a massive understatement.

After an initial wobble, he had managed to assemble his dream team. The inspection of Hartles would be carried out by the dregs of the dregs in the Ofsted Fantasy League. There were some real stars among the ranks of the inspectorate, and the majority of the rest were hardworking and committed. It took a long time to form a team of eight who were sufficiently lazy, incompetent and corrupt to fit Danny's criteria.

He would never have got anywhere without the help of Alec Pryke, his workstream supervisor back at Ofsted Towers. The not-so-former spy had been astonishingly supportive, to the point where Paranoid Danny wondered who was really in charge of Operation Outstanding. Alec gave him access to files on each of the potential candidates, files which contained personal information that no one should ever have. Danny was shocked, but that didn't stop him using the files to the full. When his chosen lead inspector suddenly became unavailable, Alec came up with an amazing replacement called Dr Jean-Jaques Mosley, whom they immediately codenamed Captain Jack. When Danny finally plucked up the courage to ask his supervisor why he was being so helpful, Alec just shrugged his shoulders and said he was doing a favour for an old friend.

Danny thought about Alec's low-key response, and several sleepless nights ensued. In the end, he decided not to worry about who was manipulating him, as long he was getting what he wanted. "Yeah, right" said the cynical voice inside Danny's head. For once, he didn't let the other voices start the usual argument. Instead, he phoned Uncle Pete, wrote a quick note to his wife, threw most of his clothes into the back of his car and headed west.

As he was a bit late, he went straight to the meeting point: an ancient-looking pub on the Sturridge side of the River Yorne or Yeorn. The Cock and Dismay was a dirty pink cob and thatch construction, much like its landlord. Uncle Pete was in the old-fashioned snug with Crispy Dave and a large man dressed in expensive-looking smart casuals.

"Bobby Two Rivers!" exclaimed Danny. "I almost didn't recognise you without the feather."

Bobby managed a morose smile. "My fifth years hate it" he told Danny, gesturing towards his new clothes "but at least they know something important is going on. Their buy-in is essential to the success of Operation Bloody Outstanding. Where else are we going to get enough bullies and cowies from?"

Danny looked blank. "Female bullies" said Bobby contemptuously. Danny could feel the anger coming off Bobby in waves. "Ours not to reason why" he spat out.

Uncle Pete looked embarrassed and said mock-confidentially to his friend the professor "Orders from above." Danny wondered who was in a position to give Pete orders.

Uncle Pete quickly changed the subject. "Who wants a pint of the Cock's well known ale?"

When it arrived, Danny took a deep draught of his pint, and he regretted it immediately. When the coughing and spluttering had died down, Pete clapped Danny on the back and laughed. "I didn't say it was well known for being good."

"So is this the inner circle for Operation Outstanding?" Danny asked anxiously.

"Don't worry" soothed Pete "it's your gig. We're here to help you. We can't have the whole staff room in on the secret. There are teachers here I don't trust, and we've got our fair share of homo crapiens. All the rest of the staff know is what was in the letter we gave the kids to take home to their parents. So they are aware there's going to be an Ofsted inspection and" Pete added, his eyes brimming with tears of mirth, "it's set for the second week of February."

Pete's voice trailed off as he joined in with the laughter. But Danny sat there stony-faced, waiting for them to finish.

"Would someone please tell me why those dates are so bloody hilarious" he asked heatedly. "Is there some kind of Valentine's Day ritual where a virgin is sacrificed to Lamrack, the great god of mutton?"

This time, the laughter was more inclusive, but that didn't stop Pete from changing the subject.

"By the way, you can cancel your booking at the Catflea Hotel, or whatever it's called." Uncle Pete told him proudly. "You have free lodgings with Señora Prowse, luxury B&B, courtesy of Don Ron. You haven't lived until you've tried her Full Spanish Breakfast. Phil Rossall moved out this morning, when one of those houses up at Bradley Stoke suddenly became available."

"That's convenient" said Crispy Dave.

"Sodding serendipitous" Bobby Two Rivers mumbled into his pint, still aggrieved at having to change his image.

By way of explanation, Uncle Pete confided in Danny "We keep getting these cryptic missives from on high. They come in the form of handwritten letters on Hartles Hall notepaper in the Jefe's distinctive scrawl, but in perfect English,"

"Jefe?" Danny asked.

Pete smiled. "Sorry, Prof. The boss, the headmistress. Her PA was devastated. The main part of her job was to liaise with the Jefe and act as an interpreter. Not surprisingly, she swore blind there was no way that the Head could possibly have written those notes, even though they were definitely in the boss's handwriting."

"And then she disappeared" Bobby Two Rivers chipped in. "The secretary, I mean, not the Head. One day she was beavering away in the school office, the next day all that was left of her was a bunch of keys and a note. Apparently, she had come into some money, and had gone to Australia to start a new life. She made some anatomically-challenging suggestions as to where to stick her notice period. She should fit right in down under, no pun intended."

After a contemplative pause and a few punishing swigs of Cock's Ale, Uncle Pete resumed the story.

"Anyway, the upshot is that we have a new Acting Head of Office, in the lumpy shape of Doktor Doktor Liesl von Wotsits. She seems to be the latest addition to the Operation Outstanding team, if that's what we are. But we have all been awaiting your orders. You're the boss and we all want to support you."

"Okay Okay" Danny protested. "There's no need to lay it on with a trowel. So who exactly is in this group?"

"Apart from the four of us" answered Pete "there's Ginny Reeves, Phil Rossall, the inevitable Molly Stidworth, the inscrutable Mistress Sicknote, the indescribable Double Doctor Liesl and our new permanent Chair of Governors Jan Ridd."

"No Mop Bucket?" Danny enquired.

"No" said Crispy Dave, getting unsteadily to his feet. "I suppose it's time for another pint."

"Oh no it isn't" the chorus responded.

Señora Prowse was determined to spoil her new guest. Waiting for him by the cosy fire was a plate of buttered scones.

"You must be famished after the evil drink" observed the frail-looking octogenarian.

"Sorry, are you tea total?" Danny enquired.

"Heavens, no" she laughed. "I meant the beer up the Cock and Dismay. I remember the late Señor saying it was evil. He used to like going to pubs, before he went abroad."

"Oh" said Danny "where did he go?"

The Señora chuckled "No, Professor. He went abroad: he got fat. People around me always seem to get fat." She pointed to a wall covered in framed photographs, unusually displayed as Before and After portraits.

Danny's accommodation was luxurious, and he had the whole of the second floor to himself. One of the smaller bedrooms had been converted into an office, complete with a large pinboard, like you see in police dramas. He set up the computer equipment Stuart had helped him choose and put his papers into the filing cabinet. No more unproductive sleepless nights for Danny Duckworth. Operation Outstanding now had its nerve centre. "This is where the magic happens" Danny said out loud, not at all pompously.

Chapter 18 – Father Pyrex and the Illegitimates

Danny Duckworth was ridiculously happy. Who knew that dedicating his days and a good part of his nights to the twin gods of Cut and Paste could be so darned satisfying? He felt like a toddler on his birthday: he was getting lots of lovely presents, but nothing was more exciting than playing with the packaging. The system Danny had set up for writing Hartles School's policies was providing him with hours of bubble wrap fun.

Following Stuart's advice, Danny had obtained an electronic copy of the Ofsted Inspection Handbook and immediately made another copy of the Policies section. As Stuart had said, he now had a template for all the policies the perfect school should have. All he had to do was rephrase the handbook descriptors of the ideal policy to make it look like it had been written by Hartles School for Hartles School.

Even Danny had no idea how many policies there should be, if a school wanted to satisfy the paperlust of the elves of Ofsted Towers. Hartles had a professor of Education working full time on them. Danny wondered how any normal school could cope with all this bureaucracy and still have the time and energy for other activities, like teaching.

The Stealth Inspector

Danny was pleased he was using the handbook as a checklist, because he didn't have to wrack his brains for a full set of required topics. For schools, who of course had no access to the inspectors' handbook, the selecting of topics must have been an absolute living nightmare. Danny had no such problems. In just a few days and nights of creative rewriting, he had the core of a teacher's handbook that would impress the socks off the inspectors.

Danny was particularly proud of his risk assessment tool. Using the template provided, a member of staff wishing to take a group on a trip abroad, for instance, received guidance on how to identify potential dangers, estimate their degree of risk on the handy Scared Shitless Scale, suggest appropriate action and generally cover their backs. The idea was that you would be prepared in the event of a bear attack, a lost passport, a fall from a helter-skelter or an outbreak of typhoid fever. Danny suspected that any potential benefit of this process would be cancelled out when the teacher decided that this was not a good time for a school trip after all.

The bulk of the policies were much more straightforward and easier to adapt from the Ofsted manual. Danny was particularly proud of the way he had made them look like they were specific to Hartles School and the needs of Oxbridlesturridge. The reader would be left in no doubt about where the school stood on bullying, money laundering, petty theft, pornography, obesity, feminine hygiene,

158

disaster preparedness, homophobia and thirty-four other topics. He proudly showed the drafts to Uncle Pete, who was gratifyingly impressed. He did, however, surprise his friend by requesting one extra policy on extreme weather emergencies. He was keen to stress that he was not talking about disasters here, but about how the school should minimise the disruption caused by bad weather.

Pete noticed the puzzled expression on Danny's face and said in a jovial tone "Don't worry, it doesn't have to be specific to Hartles. The general tosh you churn out so well will be just fine. For the production of the teacher's handbook, I leave you in the capable hands of Gerry Butterfingers Mee."

"I noticed that Gerry is not part of the Operation Outstanding team" said Danny.

Pete seemed to find that particularly amusing. "Gerry has his uses, but when it comes to brain work, forget it. When you work one to one with him, you will come to appreciate the old equation *You plus Mee equals You.* But he is good at presentation and the computerised version of colouring in."

"I am looking forward to it" said Danny without a hint of sarcasm. "Now we have got the policies in hand, it's time to press on with Ethos. When does the voting close for the new school motto and badge?"

Uncle Pete looked a little sheepish. "I'm afraid" he admitted "the OO team couldn't think of enough half-ways decent suggestions to put to the vote of all the children and staff. So we took the easy way out and put up a suggestion box by the Reception desk under the beady eyes of the Double Doctor. Suggestions for the new school motto could either be accompanied by a sketch for a new logo or be written to go with the current design, which is supposed to portray a carrion crow perched on top of a gibbet. Motivation has been enhanced by Don Ron's offer of £100 to the winner. The deadline was end of school today."

Pete looked genuinely excited. "We can open the box and pick the winning entry in tomorrow's Operation Outstanding team meeting" he said with childlike enthusiasm. "And you can give us our marching orders for what we'll be doing in the run up to Christmas".

Danny felt happy for the first time in ages. "I'll be ready" he told his friend.

The meeting was held in the school library. The large room was ideal for audio-visual presentation, although it was virtually never used. There would be no need for PowerPoint either. That role was being usurped by a large yellow box bearing the traditional crow and gibbet motif.

The team listened respectfully as Professor Duckworth droned on about policies and compliance, but their minds were on what the motto suggestions might be, and whether they would be able to tell the staff entries from the children's.

When Danny started to talk about shared ethos, ears pricked up. Hopes were high, although notably less so among the senior teachers, whose enthusiasm had been tempered by decades of lowered expectations. The box was unlocked and papers were distributed.

"I'll make a start, shall I?" said Uncle Pete. "I've got a picture of an open mouth surrounded by the words HARTLES. ITS A RIGHT LARF". Several disappointed voices round the table echoed "Me too".

"Not one of the staff entries" Pete giggled.

"I don't think this is either" said Ginny. "It's a picture of a baseball bat with the caption 2 RIDD RULES".

"Give me that" growled Jan Ridd. "Sorry about my rudeness, Ginny. This is one for me to deal with."

Pete asked if anyone had a motto that went with the current crow and gibbet image. Molly's hand shot up and she squeaked "Sir, me sir Uncle" in a perfect parody of her eleven-year-old self. There was relieved laughter all round. "This one says FEAR THE DUCK".

"Another one here with the crow and gibbet" volunteered Bobby Two Rivers. "It sounds familiar: WHERE ELSE WOULD YOU GO?"

There were several more of that ilk before Crispy Dave announced "This is a bit different. There's a 3D outline of a diamond with the words NIL ILLEGITIMI CARBORUNDUM."

"That's Latin" said Jan Ridd. "That'll do"

"Not real Latin" Phil cautioned. "They call it Dog Latin. Made up gibberish dressed up to look like the language of ancient Rome. It means DON'T LET THE BASTARDS GRIND YOU DOWN".

"That's perfect" shouted Uncle Pete. "All those in favour . . . "

When the meeting had finished, Molly came over to where Ginny and Phil were sitting. She motioned them to follow her as she led them through the dark corridor leading to the canteen. In the kitchen, Phil could see a table with four chairs. On the table were a large hunk of Serrano ham, a slab of Manchego cheese and a bowl of fat black olives.

"Ah" said Phil. "Death by Tapas. I hope you've got a nice mature Rioja Reserva to finish us off."

Molly screwed up her face. "You just can't help it, can you? I have a nice *young* Rioja for you."

"Sounds good to me" said Ginny, keen to change the subject. "Who's the other chair for?"

"It was for Gerald" Molly replied. "But he's chickened out, as usual. Don't ask."

"So who is Pyrex" asked Phil.

"Nobody really." Molly replied. "You've got to remember that my mum is special. The normal rules of behaviour don't apply to her. She has been described as suffering from high functioning autism, with the emphasis on the word suffering. She has amazing powers, but talking to people and making friends are not amongst them. She concluded that the way to have people she could talk to was to make some herself.

"Mum approached this problem like the good Cambridge scientist she was. Her aim was to have a child with a genius for a father, so she needed a source of guaranteed A1 polymath smarty pants sperm. For various reasons, Mum failed in her attempts to go down the scientific route. She decided the only way she could find a suitable father for me was to conduct her own research, and do the experiment in vivo: that's to say, in real life."

Molly paused her narrative in order to try the food and drink. She smiled at Phil and asked him "How do you like this foodie combo, Mister Michelin?"

"Perfect" said Phil. "The classics are always the best."

She made a face at him and continued her story. "So Mum drew up a list of potential fathers and wrote them each a note inviting them to afternoon tea and sex. After a series of one-hour stands, Mum got pregnant. She had no idea who my father was, so she harked back to the original idea of a test tube baby and called him Pyrex."

"So how did you end up here?" asked Ginny.

"Mum was a brilliant biochemist, but she struggled with the role of ordinary citizen. For work and quizzes, having a phenomenal memory was a boon, but for living her life, it was a cruel curse. What she lacked was a good forgettery. Information, impressions, feelings would flood into her brain and just stay there, adding to the noise that echoed inside her head until she was screaming for quiet. She needed to simplify her life, so she spent her inheritance on a smallholding in the remotest corner of the country she could find. There she could live the life of a recluse, just her and her little bundle of joy, yours truly. She was happy to live off the land and bring me up the way she wanted. Mum even had a proper best friend for the first time in her life. Someone who really understood her needs and feelings. Someone who knocked on our door one day and asked Mum if she had any eggs for sale. Someone whom Mum knew as Ellie and I called my fairy godmother Sicknote."

"I think I prefer the name Ellie" said Ginny, but Molly was too deep into her story to be distracted.

"Mum educated me at home. She taught me everything under the sun, and I was the perfect student. I retained huge amounts of information, but I had no trouble forgetting irrelevant stuff. My fairy godmother persuaded Mum to send me to the local primary school for the final year. Sicknote persuaded her that I needed to learn how to get on with other people, and I took to it like a fish to batter. I loved making friends and acting dumb in class. And then Crispy Dave - I mean Mr Al - came to our school one day and gave us the Talk. I fell in love with him and with the idea of going to Hartles School. I pestered Mum until she agreed to let me go for a year, as long as I didn't let it interfere with my education."

"That was big of her" muttered Phil through a mouthful of ham.

"I thought so too" Molly replied. "I loved making friends in school, but I wasn't learning much, so I didn't last the year. I was taken off the school roll and resumed home schooling. But my fairy godmother gave me a wonderful present. She had persuaded the school to allow me to come in for one day a week, so long as I wore uniform and it was made clear that I wasn't truanting the rest of the time.

"Over the years, the arrangement has become looser and everyone has got used to me coming and going as I please, or rather when Mum gives me time off. I was allowed to go into any lesson, with the teacher's permission, of course. I joined some sixth form classes. Mum approved of that, and let me sit my A-levels with them."

"That's pretty amazing for a fifteen-year-old" exclaimed Ginny. "How many have you got?"

"Seven" Molly replied. "Eight, if you include Spanish."

Ginny let out a low whistle of appreciation and asked "Why wouldn't you count Spanish?"

"Hartles doesn't do Spanish" Molly said "which is ironic, considering a girl can't walk down Market Street without being accosted by some testosterone cowboy shouting at her in ropey Spanish."

Suddenly, Phil became very animated. He stared at Molly intensely and blurted out "So who did teach . . ."

But Ginny interrupted him. "Hold on a minute. You are telling us this story as if you're an only child, but you have a brother and a sister."

"Mother Earth and Twerpy Terry are adopted, unofficially at any rate." Molly's relief at the change of subject was plain for both to see. Although my beautiful sister was a bit old for adoption. They were refugees from a hippie commune that went horribly wrong. Sicknote asked Mum to take them in and, as you know by now, you don't say no to Mistress Sicknote. It's a long story, and I think we are just about finished for today."

But Phil was not finished. "And did Sicknote ask you to answer all our questions?" he whispered. Molly nodded miserably and Phil asked again "Who taught you Spanish?"

"Momo did" she replied. "I was supposed to teach her English in return, but that didn't go so well. Momo is a sweet girl, but she has severe learning difficulties."

"Except she's not a girl, is she?" said Phil. "Momo's a grown woman. Momo's our Headmistress."

"I hate you" Molly shouted, getting angrily to her feet, her chair clattering to the floor behind her. Her eyes were full of anger and unshed tears. "You make everything sound so cheap. Momo has been doing a fantastic job, right up to the car crash."

Phil pounced immediately: "When was the car crash?"

Ginny put an arm around Molly's heaving shoulders and sat her down again. The girl put her arms on the table and buried her face in them.

Ginny turned to Phil and asked "What sort of a question is that?"

Molly's voice came muffled between heart-wrenching sobs: "No, it's the right question, almost."

Ginny patted Molly's back lightly and asked "So when was the car crash?"

Molly looked up miserably and said "Next Tuesday."

Chapter 19 – The changing of the guard

Phil Rossall was relieved when Tuesday came and went without news of a car crash. Going to bed that night, he thought about what Molly had told them and he was embarrassed by his credulity. How naïve had he been to believe the rantings of a hysterical teenager? Was she really saying that there was a plot to assassinate someone from Hartles School? Phil could not think of anyone ruthless enough to do such a thing. Well, ok, he thought, maybe just the one. In the warm dark of night, it seemed ridiculous that Molly was hinting at anything serious. It was probably some adolescent prank.

The phone woke him up shortly after 6 am. He was still half asleep, so he was not as surprised to hear Ginny's voice as he should have been.

"My boyfriend just woke me . . . " she began.

"That's nice" said Phil, still on automatic pilot.

"Shut up and listen" she barked in her best classroom manner. "It's all over the national news. Not the main item, but even so. Tune into local radio and ring me back when you're up to speed".

Phil was about to say something, but Ginny had hung up. "Well that certainly is news" he said out loud. "Ginny has a boyfriend."

169

The Stealth Inspector

Badger FM was the right place for wall-to-wall coverage. They had some junior reporter freezing her socks off at the North Cliffs car park. This is radio, he thought incongruously. She could be sitting in a warm studio with a nice mug of coffee and a few well-chosen sound effects. Who would know the difference?

The narrative certainly was compelling, not least because of the gaps still to be filled in. At a quarter to twelve on Tuesday night, there was an anonymous call to 999. A man said he had been up at the coast road car park directly above Sledder's Fall. The reporter described it as a "local beauty spot, which was journalese code for a horizontal jogging venue. The car park had been deserted, presumably deemed too cold by other backseat gymnasts. He had noticed the broken fence immediately. The wooden fence was all there was between the car park and a two hundred-foot drop. The anonymous caller had clambered through the hole in the fence and looked down at the turbulent water. By the fitful light of the moon, he saw something vaguely car-shaped bobbing around in the freezing sea.

Phil thought about it for a while before ringing Ginny back. "I'll get straight to the point" he announced. "Tell me about the boyfriend."

"Come on, Phil" Ginny replied "you're not taking this seriously."

Phil sighed. "Taking what seriously? There appears to have been a tragic accident on North Cliffs last night. Probably some amorous couple, one of whom kicked the handbrake in the throes of passion. What has that got to do with either of us?"

"If you raised your sights out of the gutter for a moment," Ginny snapped back "you would see that there was a car crash on Tuesday, exactly as Molly had predicted."

"And what precisely were we supposed to do with that information?" asked Phil. There was silence on the line, before he said "I agree with you. Let's just turn up for work as usual and we'll see what happens from there."

Hartles was a hive of activity that morning, and education had little to do with it. Teachers and children alike couldn't resist the temptation to indulge in idle speculation and gossip mongering. There was a special assembly for the whole school, in which the pupils were told by their Uncle Peter that there was nothing to link the story with Hartles School, but if anyone knew anything that would help the police, they should tell a teacher or Doktor Doktor Liesl in the Office. Some of the older pupils were scratching their metaphorical heads about the way Uncle Pete had sought to distance the school from whatever had happened on Tuesday. The conspiracy theories had not focused on the school, but Uncle Pete's denial was like a red rag to a bull.

Pete asked if anyone had a question, and one sproglet's arm shot up.

"Yes. Jenny" said Pete.

"Please, Uncle. Who should we go to when Doctor Liesl isn't here?"

Uncle Pete said nothing, The silence was starting to get embarrassing, until the other deputy took over. Gerry Mee smiled down at Jenny and said "Don't you worry about the Double Doctor. She's always here. She practically lives here."

But Jenny was not to be fobbed off. She continued "She's not in school this morning, and the Cardboard Car is not in her parking spot."

Gerry Mee uttered some soothing platitudes about Liesl's imminent reappearance before dismissing the children to a day of rumours, fuelled by not one but two official denials.

The police officers who came to the school at lunchtime were not the local bobbies. Alice, one of the school's part-time receptionists, described them as "proper coppers from down Exeter, with fancy cars and nee-naws". They talked to the two deputies in the Head's office for the best part of an hour, and when they emerged, there were grey faces all round. Uncle Pete called a staff meeting after school.

Jan Ridd, in his capacity as Chairman of Governors, took charge of the meeting. He didn't go into detail on the discovery of the broken fence or the sighting of a car in the sea at the bottom of the cliff.

Jan continued "At about ten thirty this morning, someone at Hartles Hall reported our headmistress as a missing person. Sorry if this sounds a little sketchy, but it has been filtered through several policemen".

Jan Ridd's dislike of the police was well known, and entirely reciprocal. "Normally" he said "when someone is reported missing, our boys in blue wait several days before they do nothing. But, given the high profile of the case, they contacted the Jefe's work and friends, which didn't take long. Gerry here passed on our concerns about Liesl. Meanwhile, police divers have examined the wrecked car and found nothing of interest. The vehicle is being recovered, and the plan is to take it to Yeorn Quay by first light tomorrow."

Staff meetings at Hartles were normally pretty rowdy affairs, but when Jan paused for a sip of water, you could hear a pin drop. Uncle Pete continued to say nothing, and to look as if he would rather be anywhere else.

Jan pressed on: "It may be jumping the gun a bit, but there's to be an extraordinary meeting of the governors tomorrow morning.

"Aren't they all?" enquired one wit, but he barely raised a smile. Phil Rossall assumed that everyone was thinking the same as he was. Jumping the gun *a bit?* It sounded more like finishing the 100 metres before the B of Bang.

For those people lucky enough to be members of the Operation Outstanding team, the confusion didn't last long. They sat around the conference table in the head's office that evening. Uncle Pete was in charge, and he looked as if a great weight had been lifted from his shoulders.

"Welcome one and all" he began, "especially to our dear friend Gerald, who is sort of new to all this."

This was the first time Phil had noticed a small middle-aged man, who was sitting next to Molly, who had one hand resting companionably on his shoulder. He was wearing a smart grey suit and all the trimmings. Phil thought Gerald looked like a mourner at a wedding.

Gerald inclined his shining bald head in acknowledgment and Uncle Pete continued: "But first, some news about our other escapee. Molly, could you do the honours?"

Molly beamed and said "A few hours ago. I received a phone call from my friend Momo, our former headmistress. She sounded in good spirits for someone whose lifeless body had been swept out to sea, never to be seen again. She is safely on board the ferry from Plymouth, bound for Santander in northern Spain. I passed on your message, Uncle, expressing our thanks for her service to Hartles School and our best wishes for her future."

Molly sat down abruptly. There was a spontaneous round of applause, but it was unclear who or what it was for.

Pete took over the reins again. "Tomorrow, the governors" he said, with a nod toward Jan Ridd "are meeting to appoint an Acting Head."

"There's only one candidate" Jan added, "so we will only take a couple of hours and half a dozen bottles of Don Ron's best Fino."

"Somehow" said Ginny "I don't see our Uncle Pete as a headmaster."

Pete clearly took this as a compliment. "Which is why" he went on "the single name on the governors' list does not belong to me but to the other deputy."

The ensuing silence was broken by Crispy Dave, who roared "Oh well, at least we will be safe in the hands of Gerry Butterfingers Mee."

"That's right" declared Pete, completely immune to sarcasm. "Gerry is the perfect man for the job. He's a master of plausible deniability. He has spent his whole working life covering up the fact that he doesn't know what's going on. So long as we keep him in a permanent state of ignorance, he will cover all the angles, like a good goalkeeper. So our Acting Head will now be out of the Operation Outstanding loop, which is why he is honouring us with his absence today."

"But how will Gerry know what to do and say to the Ofsted inspectors?" asked Bobby Two Rivers.

"He won't" replied Pete "but his Personal Assistant will. Tomorrow, we will appoint a new PA. Over to you, Gerald."

The dapper, shiny-pated figure got to his feet. His demeanour was slightly camp, and he spoke in a mellifluous tenor voice.

"For those of you who don't know my story," he began, "my name is Gerald Conran, or rather that's my stage name. You won't recognise me from the telly. I tend to play roles like third corpse from the left. Very lucrative but not exactly fulfilling. My heart is in the West End theatre, in developing comedic characters and playing modern British farce."

The OO team sat in silence, enthralled by Gerald's beautiful voice. Suddenly, Phil Rossall stood up and pointed an accusing finger at Gerald. "I know you" he announced dramatically. "You're Double Doctor Liesl".

Most of the group stared at him with pity. Ginny Reeves threw her pen at him.

"Spots on, Duckling" said Gerald joyfully. "Give that man a Sachertorte! I didn't think I could fool a German-speaker for so long. I was getting quite fond of the old bat, but the costume sessions were becoming tiresome. Way too much infrastructure.

So imagine the relief when I found out we could chuck her down a cliff in an empty car and consign her to a watery grave.

"So I became Gerald again, a washed up old actor with chronic stage fright. But fortunately, I have only had to be Gerald for a few hours. From today on, I am the shiny-headed Alan Derbyshire, soon to be anointed the headmaster's new PA. Thanks to Liesl, I know the school inside out, but she was a bloody awful German teacher. As Alan, I will make amends for that and help you, my friends, get the Outstanding grade you so desperately need."

Gerald/Alan raised his glass and proposed a toast: "To Liesl, recently departed, *Gott sei Dank*".

When the clamour had died down, Sicknote said in a quiet but steely voice "Now perhaps we can get on with the work we need to do before the Ofsted jackboots come marching into school."

Chapter 20 – Gerry and the P45s

Preparing Hartles School for a routine Ofsted inspection would have been challenging enough, Professor Danny Duckworth thought. But to bring such a patchily adequate school up to a level deemed Outstanding by a team of expert critics seemed impossible. One of the voices inside Danny's head said they might as well try to get the canteen a Michelin star while they were at it. A shadow of Danny's old anxieties crossed his semi-conscious mind. But then he found himself smiling, as he remembered that they only had to give Hartles School the *illusion* of excellence for a few days in February, and that was still a long way away.

But February wasn't that far away. He was responsible for implementing the Operation Outstanding plan, and the target date of Monday 11 February was hurtling towards him.

Danny had been far from idle. By the time he was forced to take a break for Christmas, he had finished drafting the teachers' handbook, and he was onto the staff training programme. But, for the next two weeks, there would be no staff to train. He had run out of excuses. Time to face the wife again.

As soon as the new year bells had finished ringing, Danny was on the road again, back to his happy place, his desk at Casa Prowse. Every member of staff now had a handbook outlining what they should say and do during the Ofsted inspection. Acting Head Gerry Mee had done a great job collecting all the evidence the inspection team could possibly want, He had really gone to town on beautifying the staff handbook, and Danny felt that Gerry had earned the right to have his little joke: into the back of each folder, he had slipped a copy of a P45 form.

For Danny, January went by in a swirl of frenzied activity. He and the newly christened A-Team of the Acting Head and his PA Alan Derbyshire completed all the remaining staff interviews. As Mistress Sicknote observed in one of their Operation Outstanding meetings "Our colleagues have had the fear of God put well and truly up them".

Alan Derbyshire took care of all the logistics and seemed to be responsible for everything Gerry Mee said and did. He was certainly more active than his previous incarnation as Doktor Doktor Liesl. Danny was grateful for the help, but he wondered who was giving Alan his orders. It certainly wasn't him. His money was on Sicknote.

But he really didn't care what deal Alan had struck with the two County Councils, why he had registered Hartles Hall as a hotel and promptly filled it full of closed-circuit surveillance equipment, or why he had employed the two cameramen and two of the "actresses" from Jan Ridd's burgeoning porn empire.

All the pupils had a new badge sewn neatly over the old one on their jacket, and everyone had had a series of lessons on the school motto *Nil Illegitimi Carborundum*, which they were told meant *Steadfast Under Pressure*. They learned how to behave when the inspectors were around, what questions they were likely to ask, and how they should respond. Uncle Pete told them if anyone was struggling with these lessons, he would drop round to their house in the evening and give them some extra tuition. There were no takers.

On the surface, little else happened in January or the beginning of February. Sam the Bodger and his team of cack-handed incompetents turned up to help the caretaker fix leaks and rotting window frames. They then proceeded to make a hash of painting all the classrooms white.

The inspectors duly arrived on Sunday 10th February. Soon, the gravel drive of Hartles Hall Hotel was full. The hotel's first six guests had each decided to come by car. As the Head's PA explained to Jean Jacques Mosley, the leader of the inspection team, there was no viable public transport alternative. Alan Derbyshire was sitting in the magnificent entrance lobby, waiting to greet each member of the team. A handful of grey-faces responded to his words of welcome with stiff formality. As soon as Alan revealed his affiliation with Hartles School, he could sense the metaphorical shutters go up behind their eyes. Clearly, it was not allowed to fraternise with the enemy. One woman with an apparent empathy bypass glanced at her watch to check it was still Sunday. No wonder Danny had described them as the dregs de la dregs of the Ofsteding world.

Jean Jacques Mosley, known by all as Captain Jack, was a very different character. Unlike his stony-faced colleagues, he was gregariousness personified. Within minutes, he was living up to his piratical nickname, knocking back the booze and not paying a penny for it. He knew from their email exchange that the accommodation came at a ridiculously low rate. Alan had explained that they were the hotel's first customers and therefore eligible for a half-price deal - so Captain Jack seemed determined to spend the rest of the expenses on alcohol. With a little creative accounting, the secret was safe between Alan and the Captain's fatty liver. The barman didn't count, even when he came in the resplendent form of Don Ron Hartles. Alan was surprised how charming a host the aristocrat could be. Far from being a reclusive misanthrope, the agoraphobic Don seemed to love the presence of visitors.

One thing that should have struck the guests as odd was that they were outnumbered by the staff. In addition to the genial host, there were two young men, introduced to Captain Jack as The Twins, although one was black and the other white. Don

Ron explained that they were just finishing the wiring in the banqueting hall, and that dinner tonight would have to be room service. In addition to the cook, there were two disturbingly young-looking waitresses, who introduced themselves as Dakota and Blue. Nobody explained why they were dressed in cut-off French maid's uniforms, and Captain Jack didn't ask. When the waitresses went around to all the guests' bedrooms to deliver the trays of food, the camera crew followed at a distance. The twins Rick and Mick already had good footage from the covert cameras. They just needed some linking shots before they went with the girls to a room in the other wing of the Hall. There they could record the more familiar scenes, complete with the requisite squeals and groans.

Day One of the inspection was a beautiful sunny day, but with a hard frost. After a Full Spanish Breakfast, half the inspection team took up Alan's offer and walked for ten minutes to the school. "Here we go" thought Alan, as they entered the building, "let battle commence."

Chapter 21 - There's no plan A

To say that the first day of Hartles School's Ofsted inspection was an anti-climax was like describing the last world war as a spot of local difficulty. From his little office behind the school library, Professor Danny Duckworth watched the mediocrity of his chosen school unfold like a slow-motion train crash. He knew the paperwork had gone down a storm, and the score card had started with a couple of Excellents. The mood music coming through Danny's headset from the inspection team's allocated room was pretty positive. Even the interviews with small groups of pupils about the school's ethos were going well. Most of the children had learned their lines by heart. When the rotund Mrs Brimble asked about the significance of the school badge, they said the motto meant they should be steadfast under pressure and the diamond showed how beauty and strength could be born under the greatest possible pressure. Danny mimed sticking two fingers down his throat but Mrs Brimble seemed happy enough with the answers. However, she did appear to be bemused by Jane Rowley's assertion "It means the duck is dead." Nor did she know what to make of Ian Smiley's response "I am not going to tell you I don't know, am I? I don't want Uncle to drop by for a chat, do I?" Fortunately for Danny, the inspector was like the area on a Venn diagram where laziness and incompetence intersected. Danny listened in to her feedback to the team leader, Captain Jack, and the professor was happy at what he heard. Danny allowed himself a smug smile.

It didn't take long for the smile to curdle into a scowl. The problem was that the teachers at Hartles School weren't very good. He dipped in and out of lessons on his console, including the ones observed by inspectors, and the only things he could grade as excellent were the children's behaviour and participation. Danny spent the rest of the day searching for outstanding lessons. Of the sixteen assessed by Ofsted, ten were on CCTV, and Danny was hard pressed to find any of them worthy of the highest mark. These recordings shone a cruel spotlight on the staff's mediocrity. Perversely, the only thing that cheered him up was the catalogue of errors displayed by the inspectors themselves. The cameras had caught them chatting with children when the teacher was speaking, eating and drinking during the lesson, arriving late and leaving very early. Alec Pryke had promised him a sorry bunch of losers, and they did not disappoint. For a moment, Danny wondered what an evil genius of a film editor like Jan Ridd could make of these scenes. He was soon back to gloom, though, as he contemplated telling the Operation Outstanding group that their teachers were not up to standard.

Danny did not have long to wait. Barely an hour after home time, the OO team assembled in the library. Danny gave them his tale of woe and showed them a few snippets from the covert filming. He was confused by the reaction of his audience. They did not seem to be at all concerned about the staff's inability to excel. They were clearly more interested in the pictures than in what he had to say. When he had finished his report, there was silence, as if everyone was holding their breath.

"Come on " Sicknote said "we all know what this means. It's time for Plan B. And we only have two days of the inspection left."

"There you go again " groaned the paranoid professor "knocking off days at the end of this week. Please let me into your secret, and for heaven's sake, don't just laugh at me."

They laughed quietly and Jan Ridd said "Fortunately, we already have a lot of the materials we need. Alan is in the Head's office with Captain Jack, going through the Captain's voluminous security file with him as we speak. Once Jack has been turned, as the spy folks say, he will accept and implement the inspection timetable we have written for him. He will also agree to the interviews for the other five members of his team, and you can leave the rest to me and my family."

Jan went on to outline the plan to extend the film *Bringing Up Oxbridge* to include lots of footage from the Ofsted inspection. Uncle Pete here will play his usual role as Lord of Misrule. I will edit the film on Thursday and then hand it to Sicknote for her to weave her magic."

Danny rose furiously to his feet and shouted "This has been the plan all along. Everything else was just window dressing."

"Very necessary, though" soothed Pete. "You have given us proof in black and white of our excellence in two areas. You can sit back and watch the mayhem."

Danny didn't want to see any mayhem but he was intrigued by the sight of Uncle Pete charging round the place, followed by a gaggle of Ridds. On his way out, Danny saw Captain Jack crawling out of the head's office, ashen-faced and utterly broken.

Chapter 22 - The weather lends a hand

Professor Danny Duckworth got up dull and early. He trudged his way to school and stopped when he saw a crowd gathering in the playground. Everyone was pointing and looking at the roof of the tuck shop. On its slate tiles was daubed in white paint the word JACKANNORy. Two of the inspectors had turned up early, and the children were only too keen to tell them about the history teacher who ran the tuck shop and told his classes tall stories about his heroic deeds. The twin cameramen Rick and Mick Ridd filmed the scene from a safe distance, in line with their role for the next two days. They made sure to get plenty of shots of the inspectors, establishing their presence at the scene of the incident. The day had started on a high for the two-tone twins: they had got a clear shot of one Ofsted inspector pointing towards the graffiti and saying something to his colleague, whereupon they both shook with laughter. Rick was looking forward to dubbing some suitable words in to match the movement of their lips. It was surprisingly easy and very satisfying.

The inspectors did not have to follow Captain Jack's suggested itinerary, but he knew they would. He also knew that the inspection schedule foisted upon him by that bastard Alan Derbyshire was there for a reason, but he had no idea what the reason was. He was sure that, woven into the fabric of dull but competent lessons, were the ones his team was supposed to witness.

One of those targeted teachers just had to be Mrs Roby. Most of the time, the diminutive Biology mistress spent her lessons sitting behind the desk, reading out from a book on her lap. The only time Mrs Roby ventured out from her lair was to use the blackboard, when she sometimes had no choice but to take the book with her. The fifth-year bottom set Integrated Science class liked it that way. They liked her and generally behaved well, apart from the incident of the ticked book. There had been an exercise book check recently, and one boy's book was gratifyingly full of Mrs Roby's little red ticks. Unfortunately, one of them was right next to the title *Whore Moans in Puberty*.

Today, however, the gloves were off. The drawer of the teacher's desk had been unlocked and the precious book had been doused in glue. After a few attempts at freeing and opening her book, Mrs Roby realised that she would have to teach the lesson herself. Danny, watching on CCTV from the safety of his little office, had some idea what was about to happen. He doubted the same could be said of Mr Angus Teich, a senior inspector of schools, who could clearly be seen napping at the back of the classroom, fighting off the effects of his

The Stealth Inspector

Full Spanish Breakfast. Danny was keen to assess this inspector and write up his report for the OO team. He planned to do this for each of the six inspectors, but he had particularly low hopes for Mr Teich. At least he was awake now and writing notes while nodding and smiling. The children were heads down, writing furiously in their jotters. All seemed fine until Mrs Roby wrote the title THE HUMAN BRIAN. She drew a cross section of a brain, with lines inside it to show its key areas. She drew a line to the outer cap surrounding the other parts and labelled it CORTEX. She said a little about grey matter and its function in memory.

And then she froze. The pupils were unnaturally quiet as they watched her go back to her desk and scrabble around in the drawer. Eventually, she gave up and returned to the blackboard and said "This is the stem, where the brain meets the spinal cord. This is the perineal gland, the funicular and the sternum. And this large chamber is the cervix."

Danny got tired of car crash TV, but he was glad he stayed with this lesson to the bitter end. The inspector watched the orderly dismissal of the class before shaking the teacher's hand and saying something inaudible. Danny had the feeling that the Ridds would supply a suitable soundtrack.

Danny watched several lessons for the rest of the day and he found little of interest. Apart from the humming lesson. Ms Walsh was a young maths teacher with tenuous control of her classes. She liked to give lots of tests to give her some respite from the constant battle of wills. So it was no surprise that the lesson to be observed by the inspector turned into a big test. Under Ofsted rules, this should not have happened, but all her lessons that week seemed to be wall-to-wall testing. So Percy Brindle-Jones, her designated assessor, decided to sit at the back of the room and watch the test. There was utter silence in the room as the teacher gave instructions and the thirty second-year students bowed their heads over their papers. From somewhere towards the back of the class came a tiny whining noise, like a mosquito trapped in a distant net. For a long time, this sound had the room to itself. Then a low fly-like buzzing was added to the teacher's soundtrack of misery. The noise rapidly reached a crescendo as thirty juvenile voices produced the wailing of a banshee. The children kept their heads down as the teacher fled to the relative safety of her desk, where she sobbed her heart out. Throughout this whole sorry episode, the inspector sat there impassively, tight-lipped, seemingly absorbed by whatever was on his clipboard. Danny was sure he knew how Jann Ridd would make it look like the inspector had started the humming.

At the height of the cacophony, a little girl put her hand up and shouted "Miss, finished". When no response was forthcoming, she walked over to the teacher's desk and said "Finished, Miss". Getting no response, she added "Would you like some chocolate?"

At the Operation Outstanding meeting that evening, there was a feeling of excitement in the air. Uncle Pete was chairman, and he passed on Jan Ridd's apologies. Apparently, he was moving his editing equipment down to Hartles Hall to make his part of the operation "weatherproof". This got a warm chuckle from the team. Danny did not even bother to ask. Pete also said that the editors had plenty of great shots of the inspectors for Jan to work with.

Pete showed them some of the footage from the "inspector interviews". He began with Captain Jack's grilling the night before. Gerry Mee just sat there and played his role as silent Acting Head. His secretary, Alan Derbyshire, did all the talking. Gone were the kindly tones of Doktor Doktor Liesl. Gerald's new incarnation Alan was like a dog with a bone. He opened the security file on Jack, and grilled him on every dubious detail. Alan was utterly ruthless and he soon had enough dirt for a successful blackmail campaign. Jack was wanted in five countries to face allegations varying from fraud to inappropriate touching, none of which showed up on his vetting form. When he thought the Captain could take no more, Alan switched the subject and showed Jack a printout of a bank statement. Jack recognised it as his own. Alan pointed to the last deposit, which was for £10,000 from Hartles School.

"Care to explain this?" asked Alan . "Looks like a bribe, doesn't it? And don't even think of moving the money. That would just add money laundering to your list of charges."

Uncle Pete showed the OO team excerpts from other interviews. They went along similar lines. Danny was amazed how much incompetence, venality and sheer criminality could be packed into six apparently respectable-looking individuals. Still, Danny was glad they had the bank account scam to fall back on. The presence of ten thousand pounds in their account would be both tempting and hard to explain away. Nevertheless, Operation Outstanding relied on the participation of all the inspectors. One rogue inspector could still derail the whole enterprise. This film had better be pretty darned good.

Danny, along with the rest of the OO team had received an invitation to a "lock-in party" that Tuesday night at the Hartles Hall Hotel. Danny asked what the lock-in party was, and Crispy Dave replied "It's going to snow tonight. It's come early this year. It usually comes on Valentine's Day. You should get to the Hall by 9pm if you don't want to miss the fun. Or freeze to death. A proper little Agatha Christie lock-in. Once we are all in there, we are not going anywhere for a few days."

Danny didn't believe a word of it. He thought Dave might have slipped back into pantomime mode. Nevertheless, he checked the weather forecast before he walked over to the Hall. Sure enough, for this corner of the temperate South West, the worst they could predict was heavy rain.

But, scarcely five minutes into his short walk, it became bitterly cold, and he was suddenly engulfed by a serious blizzard. It was hard going, but he got to the top of the Hall drive when the weather did something weird. It stopped snowing, and Danny was immediately doused by bucketloads of freezing rain. Before he dived into the sanctuary of the hotel lobby, he saw that his coat was covered with a thick layer of ice.

Chapter 23 - Outstanding

"Beautiful, isn't it?" said Ginny Reeves, looking out of a window of the Hartles Hall Hotel at the ice-bound town of Oxbridge.

"It's certainly unusual " replied Phil Rossall. "Every surface is covered in two inches of sparkling ice. Nothing is moving out there. And the inspectors are at our mercy for a day or two."

The gong sounded, and everyone went to the great hall for the film premiere. The inspection team filed in like lambs to the slaughter. Jan Ridd looked exhausted as he introduced the film. He and his editors had been up all night, turning the old footage from *Bringing Up Oxbridge* into a farce of epic proportions. New material from the covert filming of the Ofsted inspection had been interwoven by a fiendishly-skilled editor into an irresistible story of how these particular inspectors ruined Hartles School. An extra soundtrack was supplied by gifted mimics from Jan's porn production team who were brilliant at putting words into other people's mouths. The combined effect was crude but irresistible. The faces of every member of the Ofsted team are clearly visible as they encourage the children to behave appallingly.

One inspector starts humming during an otherwise silent maths test. The children pick up the idea and soon the test is ruined by a deafening chorus of buzzing.

Two Ofsteders were standing in the playground. One of them appeared to be shouting instructions to a boy standing on the roof of the tuck shop. The boy was painting graffiti and the inspectors shared a laugh at the results. Then they turned their attention to a group of bullies stealing sweets from smaller children. It looked like they were egging the bullies on.

The film went on to show a bewildering display of classroom mayhem. All the scenes from the old mockumentary and the new footage were linked together by scenes involving each of the inspectors faked or taken out of context. The neutral viewer would have no difficulty identifying the Ofsted inspectors as the instigators of fiascos such as the chanting of swear words, children forced to stand in the pouring rain on a mop bucket, teenagers exposing themselves while the class makes models of their genitalia.

When the film finished, the inspectors looked shocked and demoralised. Not only were they being taken hostage by a bunch of rabid teachers, but even the weather conspired against them.

Danny Duckworth finally got the joke about the weather in mid February. Oxbridge had very little snow, but around Valentine's Day it was hit by a stonking great ice storm. The Ofsted team had nowhere to go, so they allowed themselves to be led to an improvised meeting room to write their report. Uncle Pete, that grandmaster of disguised blackmail, told them they could burn the only two copies of the film in exchange for one word at the top of their report: OUTSTANDING.

Epilogue

No one was more surprised than Danny Duckworth that the ruse had worked. Three years after the Great Con, as Danny had dubbed it, the victory over Captain Jack and his Ofsted Pirates had transformed the school and the whole town. The main change to the school was the massive poster emblazoned with the word OUTSTANDING. The staff seemed content to stay for life. Even the standard of teaching had improved a little, aided by better morale and injections of cash from Sicknote's booming business empire.

Danny thought it was only right and proper that Sicknote had profited most from the scam, as she was responsible for the whole thing in the first place. The former spy had manipulated everyone into giving her business what it needed: a secondary school in the area with the highest possible official rating. The family segment of her customer base seemed more than happy to sign up for Sicknote's discreet services. Many more people were ready to part with huge sums of money in exchange for a chance to drop out of society and live off grid for a while. She used that money to buy the town's only supermarket and the nearly derelict pottery, which she promptly handed over to Statham. The school's failed art teacher soon became a successful potter.

Still flying beneath the radar, Sicknote now had a luxury hotel and a magnificent stately home, where she lived in wedded bliss with her wife, the Marchioness. She also had Danny Duckworth. The ex-professor had stayed on in Oxbridge and was happily beavering away at basic admin in Sicknote's rather shadowy organisation. He still thought about teaching but only in his nightmares.

Ginny stayed on too and got married. The only one to jump ship was Phil Rossall who went off to pursue a life of mediocrity in a succession of schools across the south east of England. The town formerly known as Oxbridlesturridge flourished without the locals noticing the gradual change. It was now officially known as Oxbridge, and Uncle Pete was still mayor. He seemed set for life. People associated him with the town's new prosperity and Pete was not in a hurry to disabuse them.

Ofsted had no idea it had been duped but it seemed to have learned from the experience gathered during these trial inspections. It soon became a major pillar of government education policy but Danny thought it was built on shifting sands. His enthusiasm for transparency and accountability had evaporated in Oxbridge's soggy air. Now he considered the whole thing a colossal waste of time. Not just the Ofsted thing but teaching in general. He looked across the pub table at Uncle Pete and thought he had been right all along. Education was a necessary evil but it wasn't for him. He raised his glass of dead dog for a toast and said "Nil illegitimi carborundum. Don't let the bastards grind you down!"

The Stealth Inspector

Other books by Phil Rossall:

Motor Neurone Disease the Fun Bits

See also:

Phil's blogs at:

https://livingwithmotorneuronediseasethefunbits.home.blog/

Phil's vlogs, his blinking, marathon and other videos at:

https://www.youtube.com/channel/UCH5vP_Z5nQq5Qf5XV2KrUPg

Phil's Just Giving page at:

https://www.justgiving.com/fundraising/Phil-Rossall4

The Stealth Inspector

Printed in Great Britain
by Amazon

21066918R00120